'You were impressive back there,' Ivy told Olivia. 'Cold as ice. You should be a vampire!'

'Yeah, go to vampire school or something!' Olivia joked. Ivy slowed to a stop and watched her twin pull ahead.

You have no idea how close to the truth you are, Ivy thought. *One of us really might be about to enrol at a vampire academy.*

Sink your fangs into these:

🦇

🦇

Sienna Mercer

MY SISTER THE VAMPIRE

TWIN SPINS!

EGMONT

With special thanks to Chandler Craig

For Mom and Dad, for everything

EGMONT

We bring stories to life

My Sister the Vampire: Twin Spins! first published in Great Britain 2012
by Egmont UK Limited
239 Kensington High Street
London W8 6SA

Copyright © Working Partners Ltd 2012
Created by Working Partners Limited, London WC1X 9HH

ISBN 978 1 4052 5984 2

3 5 7 9 10 8 6 4 2

A CIP catalogue record for this title is available from the British Library

Typeset by Avon DataSet Ltd, Bidford on Avon, Warwickshire
Printed and bound in Great Britain by the CPI Group
49531/3

EGMONT LUCKY COIN

Our story began over a century ago, when seventeen-year-old
Egmont Harald Petersen found a coin in the street.

He was on his way to buy a flyswatter, a small hand-operated
printing machine that he then set up in his tiny apartment.

The coin brought him such good luck that today Egmont has
offices in over 30 countries around the world. And that lucky
coin is still kept at the company's head offices in Denmark.

Chapter One

*O*omph!

    Olivia Abbott winced as a pair of shiny black combat boots squashed the sparkly polish of her freshly painted toenails.

'Sorry.' Olivia's twin sister, Ivy, smiled sheepishly, regaining her balance. Her boots might have been gothtastic, but they were also lethal in a crowd as squished-in as this one. Olivia helped steady her sister. With the whole student body crammed into the assembly hall waiting to hear Principal Whitehead's big school announcement, it was all Olivia and Ivy could do to keep from being knocked flat.

Olivia felt her phone buzz twice from inside her pocket – a new email! It had been days since Camilla's last Paris update. Camilla was a loyal friend to Olivia and Ivy, even if she was a bit, um . . . eccentric. All anyone needed to know about Camilla was that she was creative with a capital 'C'. She'd organised their school production of *Romeo and Juliet*, giving it an interesting cyborg update, and she'd become really involved on the film set when Hollywood had come to Franklin Grove. Now she was in Europe, on holiday with her family, soaking up the culture there.

Olivia wormed her fingers into the pocket of her jeans and pulled her phone out, squinting at the screen:

Olivia,
Please say you have finished the last installment of the Cyborg Trilogy. *It's at least five times better than*

Random Access. *We must discuss* ASAP.
Camilla

P.S. Paris is cool. We should work on our French accents.

In every message Camilla had sent from her vacation, she'd seemed just as interested in the latest Coal Knightley book as in exploring one of the most romantic cities on the planet. Only Camilla could dig great culture *and* get lost in a book at the same time!

A confident, familiar voice was chattering away behind Olivia. 'I overheard a couple of the teachers talking, so *I* already know what the big announcement is.' Olivia turned to look. Blonde ponytail, extra-shiny lip gloss, and a manicured hand propped on one hip. It was Charlotte Brown, Franklin Grove's resident head cheerleader and diva. Of course Charlotte would have made it a top priority to be in the know about something important happening at school.

Charlotte's friend Katie was craning to listen. Her eyes were out on stalks at the possibility of the juicy gossip. What was wrong with finding out with the rest of the school?

Olivia squeezed her eyes shut. 'Don't listen, don't listen,' she whispered to herself. She didn't want the surprise of the announcement to be ruined.

'There's going to be a school dance,' Charlotte declared. 'And I heard it's going to be at the end of the summer holidays, which is killer because by then I'm guaranteed to have the perfect tan.' Trust Charlotte to think that frazzling in the sun was a good idea.

Katie squealed and clapped her hands. 'Really? You're sure?'

'Totally. Plus, it will give me plenty of time to make my yearbook film.'

Ivy and Olivia shared a surprised glance. Charlotte had been put in charge of making the yearbook film? Were the teachers crazy? If only Camilla was in Franklin Grove instead of Paris – she'd have done a much better job. 'What are the odds that she'll include any goths in that video?' Ivy whispered.

Olivia chewed her lip. Charlotte was all about pink, there was no denying it. But surely she would want to have Ivy's ultra goth-chic style gracing the yearbook video? Perhaps Ivy was being too hard on her.

'I don't know.' Olivia shrugged. 'She's been much nicer since the *Bright Stars* awards ceremony. She helped us out, remember?'

Olivia still got the jitters thinking about that night. She'd been in line to win the Brightest New Star award when Jessica Phelps, top Hollywood actress, had tried to expose Olivia's secret relationship with mega-star Jackson Caulfield.

His fans had gone batty! Luckily Olivia had won the award anyway and she'd been able to win the fans over with her acceptance speech, but speaking in front of a swarm of rabid Jackson fans was not something she'd attempt again. Not that she could blame them. It was hard not to get a little light-headed when it came to a super-cute movie star like Jackson. Her own heart gave a loop-the-loop as she thought back to their first kiss, before another thought squirmed into her head. *But what good is having a celebrity boyfriend if I never get to see him?*

Olivia and Jackson had barely laid eyes on each other since the award ceremony – he'd been busy promoting the film and she'd had to return to school in Franklin Grove. This wasn't how she'd imagined things at all when they'd stood on stage together, listening to the cheers of the audience in Hollywood. It had all felt like a dream come true. *But perhaps that's all it was*, she thought. *A dream.*

Ivy must have guessed what she was thinking because she squeezed Olivia's hand, her Midnight Mauve lips curving down. 'You're missing Jackson, aren't you?'

Olivia loved that her twin could read her emotions so well, but she didn't want to come off too needy. 'Maybe a little.' She smiled, holding up her thumb and finger an inch apart. 'But I guess I'd better get used to it. If there really is a dance, I doubt Jackson will even be able to come. Not unless Amy lets him wriggle out of his tour.'

Ivy made a sour face. Amy Teller was Jackson's manager and the chances of her letting a top star like Jackson take a break from a press tour were practically zilch.

'Hi, guys!'

Olivia beamed as she spotted Brendan and Sophia fighting their way through the crowd.

'Pardon you!' Charlotte jumped out of the

way of Sophia. 'Watch where your chunky boots are clomping!' Katie made a big show of pulling Charlotte to safety as Olivia looked on, shaking her head. *Perhaps Charlotte should save some theatrics for her yearbook film.*

The chopsticks pinning Ivy's hair in place nearly poked Olivia's eye out as she spun to greet their friends. Her slender arms wrapped around Brendan's neck, pulling him into a big hug. From the look on Brendan's face, Olivia reckoned he couldn't be happier. She remembered when she first came to Franklin Grove, and Ivy had announced with such despair, 'I'm utterly in love with Brendan Daniels.' *And look at them now!*

'We thought you were hiding from us,' Brendan joked, running a hand through his hair. It was usually shoulder-length, but had been cut shorter and shaggy last week.

'No,' said Ivy, craning up to look at her

boyfriend. 'We're just vertically challenged.'

'We were just discussing the dance,' Olivia explained to Sophia.

'Dance?' Sophia's eyes glittered.

'You-know-who spilled the beans.' Olivia hiked her thumb over her shoulder at Charlotte, whose head jerked up as if she could sense someone talking about her.

Ivy gently punched her sister. 'Olivia!'

Her twin smacked a hand over her mouth, eyes wide. 'And I've just done the same thing! You guys, I'm so sorry.'

Brendan was gazing at Ivy, a smile forming on his lips. 'It's OK. Sounds like good news to me.'

Ivy snorted. 'Yeah, I'm sure you're just itching to put on a fancy suit and waltz around the assembly hall!'

Brendan's smile faded. 'But –'

Sophia clapped her hands. 'I'm not disappointed. I have a dress I've been dying to wear!'

Olivia crossed her fingers. 'I just hope Jackson can make it back in time!'

Ivy tilted her head. 'But won't you be filming on set by the end of the summer?'

Olivia felt like smacking herself square in the forehead. 'You're right!' she squealed.

The crush of students must have been squeezing her brain. How could she forget? She'd only been looking forward to filming *Eternal Sunset* every day since she'd got the part! As soon as Jackson's press tour ended, the two of them were due to start work on a new film together.

'I guess neither of us will make it, then,' Olivia sighed. 'Shame. It would have been almost as much fun as when we all went to the Transylvanian ball together.' She lowered her voice and leaned towards Ivy. 'Without quite so many vampires!'

'And with way more bunnies,' Ivy pointed out.

'And more pink.'

Ivy scrunched her nose. 'So basically you're saying there's no way the Franklin Grove dance could be as amazing as the Transylvanian ball?'

'Come on.' Olivia nudged Ivy. 'I bet there's someone who would love to call you his date to the dance.' Olivia nodded at Brendan, who was chatting with Sophia.

Ivy blushed, glancing away. 'I just feel sorry for whoever gets stuck organising this year,' she stammered. 'I'd rather be zombified than worry about colour palettes and dance themes. *So* not my thing.'

'Oh!' Olivia hopped up and down, pointing at the front of the assembly hall. 'It's Principal Whitehead. Look! Look!'

Their principal stepped up to the small podium and the hall went quiet.

'Good morning, Franklin Grove,' he said, and cleared his throat. He fumbled with a few sheets of paper. 'I have a special announcement. As you may have heard . . .' The principal paused, making Olivia wonder if he shared her love of the dramatic. She had learned a thing or two about theatrical timing during her hours on set. At last, he spoke. 'We are going to have a school dance.'

Principal Whitehead held up his hand. 'One more thing.' The crowd was buzzing, so he lowered his mouth closer to the microphone. 'The big date for the school dance has already been decided and it is . . . next Friday!'

'Next Friday!' Charlotte shrieked. Everyone went mad. Girls grabbed their friends, jumping up and down on the spot. Boys shared alarmed glances – who would they invite to be their dates, with only a week to decide?

'Hold it, hold it.' Principal Whitehead held up his hand until the crowd settled. 'The date has been pushed forward because of essential renovations to the school building. You should also know that the school board has decided to increase security ever since some unsavoury paparazzi were found lurking in the vicinity.'

Olivia felt her cheeks flush. Their principal was talking about the photographers who'd been chasing Jackson around. He'd come to study at Franklin Grove and to be close to Olivia. That was then, but where was he now? Out on his promotional tour. Olivia tried to ignore the tightening in her chest.

The hall was filled with bunny-mania as the principal walked back to his office. Olivia and Sophia cheered along with everyone else, while Charlotte attempted to yell over the crowd, 'I knew it!' Even though the announcement hadn't been a surprise, it was still exciting. Olivia would need a new outfit and a new shade of shimmery eyeshadow and – *oh!* – she hoped Ivy would go shopping with her.

'How will I find a dress in time?' Katie cried.

Charlotte already had her mobile glued to one ear. 'Yes, this is an emergency,' she stressed into the receiver. 'No, I'll need a cut, a blow-dry, a manicure *and* a pedicure.' She cupped her hand over half the phone and mouthed to Katie, 'My tan!' Her eyes shot skywards and she flipped shut the mobile. 'Girls,' she called to anyone who was listening, 'to the beach!'

Katie looked around as if her friend had gone completely insane. 'What beach? We're hundreds of miles from the coast.'

Charlotte seemed to teeter on the edge of a breakdown. 'Um . . . strappy sandals . . . cocoa butter . . . I don't know! Let's just go!'

She rushed off, following the rest of the crowd as they left the hall. At last Olivia could breathe. Her eyes locked with a girl from her grade, Jenny, who scurried over, several big ring-binders pressed close to her chest.

'Hi, Olivia. I was wondering . . .' She ground the toe of her shoe into the floor. 'Would you like to be involved in planning the dance? You could even be chairperson if you wanted. You'd be great at it!'

Wow! Olivia hadn't so much as applied and she was being offered a lead position.

'What does a chairperson do, exactly?' asked Ivy, frowning at the piles of folders the girl was clutching.

'Chooses decorations, discusses colour schemes, themes, music and agrees it all with the principal. It's a very important position.' She waved her hand through the air. 'We have to turn all this into a dance hall by next Friday!'

Ivy shuddered. 'Not my idea of fun.'

But Olivia was already picturing the perfect centrepieces and hundreds of lights sparkling over the dance floor.

'So, do you want to?' Jenny asked, bobbing

on the balls of her feet.

'What about your film?' Ivy whispered out of the side of her mouth. Olivia's visions of a romantic dance disappeared into thin air.

'I'm sorry.' And she genuinely was. 'But I'll be too busy learning lines for my film role.'

'OK.' Jenny nodded slowly, her shoulders sagging. 'I understand. Thanks anyway.' Olivia felt a twinge of guilt as Jenny pushed her way through the other students. But this was going to be her big break. She needed to give it her all, and that meant rehearsing and re-rehearsing until she knew her lines better than she knew her own name!

As the four friends were making their way out of the hall, Olivia felt the phone in her pocket vibrate again. She slipped it out of her jeans and touched the flashing message to open it. The message was from Jacob Harker, the studio head giving Olivia her shot at Hollywood: *Olivia, my rising star, we need to catch up. Stuff's going down. Call the office. 818-350-4917.*

Olivia tugged at her sister's elbow, pulling her to a stop. 'Harker wants me to call him.'

Ivy read the message over Olivia's shoulder. 'Even for a V, that guy's a little kooky. Shouldn't he have, like, a whole squad of minions taking his calls and sending his memos? At least that's what I would do if I was that powerful.'

'Well, then, let's hope you're never that powerful,' Olivia teased. 'You'd be a slave-driver!'

'Hey!' Ivy dropped her chin and tried to shoot Olivia a death stare, but instead burst into laughter.

Olivia's stomach flip-flopped as she punched the keys for Harker's number. She couldn't believe that she, Olivia Abbott, was calling the head of a major Hollywood movie studio. How cool was that?

After three rings, the sound of Harker's

drawling voice eased on to the line. 'Duuuude, what's up?'

Olivia didn't know the proper response to that. 'Nothing . . . er . . . man,' she replied uncertainly, hoping it didn't sound weird.

'Bad news.' Harker's voice became grave. *Oh no . . . Am I getting fired? Is Jackson OK?* 'The Hollywood writers have gone on strike,' he announced.

'I'm sorry to hear that.' Olivia tried to sound sympathetic, although she had no idea what this really meant.

'No worries, my friend, but you'd better start watching reruns of your favourite shows, because it looks like it's going to be a while before you get any new episodes.'

She hadn't expected that. Olivia's mouth went dry. 'And movies?'

'Kaput, too. With no one to write the scripts around here, we're like bums on the beach.

No choice but to relax and put everything on hold.'

Olivia stopped dead. 'No more movie shoot?' It felt as if a sumo wrestler had climbed aboard Olivia's shoulders and taken a seat. She was crushed.

Ivy turned and shot her sister a worried look.

'The movie shoot will still go forward – just a year later.' Harker's voice was silky on the other end of the phone. 'Until then, we all just chill.'

Olivia couldn't tell him that she had been counting down the days until she got to work with her boyfriend.

'No problem,' she fibbed, though her voice was wobbling and she knew how miserable she must look. At least Harker couldn't see her down the phone line. 'I'll see you in a year!' She ended the call and buried the phone in her pocket.

'What's wrong?' Ivy rushed towards her. Sophia and Brendan crowded round, too.

Ivy squeezed her sister in a tight hug.

'It's bad,' Olivia told them. 'The writers are on strike and there'll be no new movie shoots and no new television episodes until it's over.' She wanted to flop to the floor.

Ivy's grip tightened so much that Olivia felt her eyes bugging. She could hardly breathe, her sister was hugging so hard.

'Ivy!' she yelped.

'Does this mean there won't be any new episodes of *Shadowtown*?' Ivy asked through gritted teeth. *Shadowtown* was a show about vampire teens, and Ivy's new guilty pleasure. She never missed an episode. 'How will I survive?' She pulled away from Olivia.

'Too bad,' said Brendan, but even Olivia could tell he didn't mean it. Ivy and Sophia both turned on him.

'What?'

He held up his hands in surrender. 'Personally, I think the show sucks. And not in a good way.'

This time Ivy did manage a death stare, and it was aimed straight at Brendan. 'How could you say that about *Shadowtown*? It's only the best show ever. This is the end of the world.' She pressed the back of her hand to her forehead and acted as though she would faint.

'For you?' Olivia interrupted. 'My film is postponed!' Not even Olivia could maintain a perky cheerleader image in the face of news this bad. 'Jackson can't come back from his promotional tour and summer holidays start today. What am I going to do? I was planning on being so busy learning my lines that I wouldn't notice he was missing.'

Ivy twirled a loose strand of her hair. 'You could get a hobby?' she suggested.

Olivia drew a sharp breath. 'That's it! You're

a genius, Ivy. Hold on one second.'

'Where are you going?' called Ivy, as Olivia dashed back down the corridor.

'I won't be long. Don't worry. I'll meet you at the gate!' She skidded around a corner and nearly collided with Jenny, who was shuffling along with her binders clasped against her chest. 'Hey!' Olivia panted. 'I was looking for you.'

Jenny shifted the enormous folders in her arms. 'You were?'

'Yes. Do you still want me to help out?'

'Oh my goodness!' Jenny's words came out in a rush. 'Absolutely!' She dumped the biggest binders on Olivia, who stumbled under the weight. 'The first committee meeting is on Sunday.' Jenny patted Olivia's arm. 'That should give you plenty of time to look those over. OK?' Olivia opened her mouth, but Jenny didn't wait to hear what she had to say. 'Great, thank you!'

Olivia could barely hold the binder, it was so

enormous. She felt herself start to tip, and before she could stop herself, she staggered on to a chair on one side of the corridor. She blinked. Jenny couldn't get away from all that paperwork fast enough. She must have *really* not wanted to organise the dance. But, wait! Was that the sound of Jenny's heels clacking on the floor? She must be coming back to help.

'Oh, um, I nearly forgot.' Jenny peered down at Olivia. 'You'll need this, too.' She balanced a clipboard on top of Olivia's pile. 'See you Sunday!'

How utterly great. Olivia tried to stand back up, struggling to manage the tower of paperwork. The files slid from her grasp and white sheets spilled across the floor.

'Stay there. That's perfect!'

Huh? Olivia looked up to see a video-camera lens in front of her nose. 'Charlotte, what are you doing?'

23

'That's great, but maybe look even more overwhelmed.' Charlotte continued filming Olivia from various angles before moving the camera to take in the mess on the floor. 'I'm so pleased you're organising this thing. I'm going to need interviews and access to behind-the-scenes footage. Got it?'

'For what?'

'For my yearbook film, silly. It's going to capture Franklin Grove School in all its glory! The good and the bad. And this –' Charlotte swooshed her hand towards the paperwork spilled on the floor – 'is definitely the bad.'

'Charlotte?' Olivia asked, sighing.

Charlotte adjusted the lens on the camera, squinting as she focused on her shots. 'Yeah?'

'How about helping me clear this up?'

Charlotte's head snapped up. 'Oh! Yeah, of course!' She stooped to lift a binder. 'Sorry about that.'

As the jumbo binder was deposited back in her arms, Olivia had to wonder: *What on earth did I just sign up for?*

Chapter Two

'Why did you agree to organise the dance?' Ivy asked her sister as they walked along the street. Olivia must have gotten bats in her brain to agree to such a thing. 'School dances are always snooze fests. They're as bad as science class!'

'Science class?' Brendan raised his eyebrows. He had relieved Olivia of her binders and was carting them up the block towards Ivy's house. Sophia had had to leave early to make her shift at the Meat and Greet Diner and Olivia and Ivy were heading for a twin sleepover at the Vegas' house. Ivy's dad had especially requested that they both stay the night, which was odd to say the least. Since when did parents suggest sleepovers?

'You know what I mean. I'd rather endure a whole day of Mister Smoothie sing-a-longs than go to the school dance!'

Brendan caught her eye and shook his head. What was his deal? All she had said was that she hated the idea of a dance! *Wait . . . Is he trying to tell me something?* Ivy clenched her fists, mentally scolding herself. *Of course!* She was totally raining on her sister's parade.

Ivy backtracked. 'You're really good at this sort of thing, though.' She tried to channel a bit of her sister's perkiness. 'I'm sure your dance will suck!'

'Thanks,' Olivia said. 'I really need the support.'

Brendan gave Ivy a small nod of approval. Where would she be without the best boyfriend ever? Hurting her sister's feelings, that was where!

Olivia giggled. 'You know, I bet you could

27

find your inner dancing queen if you did want to come.'

Ivy scrambled to change the subject. 'I hope you're not too bummed about having to miss the big cheerleader end-of-term sleepover tonight.' Even though Ivy didn't understand the draw of pompoms and bouncy ponytails, she knew her sister did. 'I mean, I love having you stay and all, but Dad was going a bit vamptator with the whole "You *must* be there" thing.'

'That's OK.' Olivia skipped over the cracks in the sidewalk. 'A twin sleepover is better than a cheerleader one any day.'

A chirpy ringtone sounded from Olivia's pocket. Ivy snorted. She wasn't sure anyone's telephone needed to sound that enthusiastic.

Olivia dug out her mobile and read the screen. 'It's Jackson! I'll be right back.' She held up one finger before bouncing ahead out of earshot.

Brendan slowed at a stop sign where two roads

intersected. 'I should be getting home.' Brendan's parents liked him to be home for dinner on time, which made sense since his mom was a fantastic cook. Ivy's mouth watered at the thought of his mother's famous hamburger patties. 'I'll see you later, though?' He pressed his lips to Ivy's cheek, a lock of his dark, shaggy hair brushing her forehead.

Ivy took the binder from him, hoping this was as close as she'd have to get to any dance planning. 'Sounds good.'

Brendan was being strangely quiet, Ivy thought, as he walked away. *He must not like the idea of a dance any better than I do! That's vamps for you.* She shrugged and jogged over to Olivia.

'Well?' Ivy asked. Olivia was putting her phone back into her pocket.

'He's in the deep south,' said Olivia. 'Where, I have no clue. I could barely hear through the bad reception.'

Ivy bumped shoulders with her sister, trying to nudge her back into her usual cheery self. 'Don't worry, you'll talk again soon.'

'I know,' Olivia groaned. 'But I miss him so much! I haven't seen Jackson since we left LA after the awards show a few weeks ago. I wish he hadn't had to go off on that promotional tour for *The Groves* straight after. It would be nice if we could talk properly at least once a century.'

'Once a century?' Ivy glanced sidelong at her twin, trying not to grin.

'You get what I'm saying. The last time I tried calling him he was being photographed on a rollercoaster at Graceland. You try having a conversation with someone surrounded by people screaming at the top of their lungs.'

'Isn't that sort of business as usual for Jackson?' Ivy pointed out. Wherever Olivia's boyfriend went, so did a swarm of screaming fans. It was enough to give any bystander a headache – especially Ivy.

They carried on walking in silence. The sidewalk started to slope up towards the top of the hill and the cul-de-sac where Ivy's house sat. The sun had dropped in the sky and now reminded Ivy of the colour of blood-orange juice, spilling reddish light on to the tops of the neighbourhood trees. She listened as her sister's jeans swooshed with hers in perfect unison.

'Hey!' she said, suddenly. 'Why am I the one left carrying these monster binders?'

Olivia cringed. 'Please, could you carry them? We don't have too far to go and my arms are dead.' She rubbed her skinny biceps.

Her twin looked so pitiful, how could Ivy say no?

'Seriously,' Olivia continued. 'My arms ache just thinking about lugging those folders again. Plus, you have vamp strength. Carrying that lot should be no big deal for you.'

Olivia was right. Ivy could carry the binders, no problem. 'OK, fine,' Ivy conceded. 'But this doesn't mean I'm going to help with the dance planning!'

Olivia placed her hand over her heart. 'I solemnly swear not to rope you into any more dance-related activities.'

'Good.' Ivy tried to look serious.

Ivy's keys jingled as she used one hand to unlock the heavy Gothic door. Inside, she dropped Olivia's dance folder on the dining-room table with a loud thud, and made a big show of shaking her arms out.

'That was rough.'

Olivia stuck out her tongue. 'Stop pretending! I thought *I* was supposed to be the actress in this family!'

'Girls, in here.' Ivy heard her father call.

The twins tramped into the kitchen. It was

strange, but now that Olivia was part of the family, this room was actually home to real human food. It still surprised Ivy when she opened the refrigerator sometimes. Vampires got all their food from the BloodMart, a secret vampire grocery store hidden in the basement of the FoodMart. Ivy couldn't remember the last time they'd had a vegetarian in their home pre-Olivia.

'Hi,' said a familiar voice. It was Lillian, leaning on the kitchen counter, looking casual-fabulous as usual, in a black turtleneck and skinny jeans tucked into her stiletto-heeled ankle boots.

Ivy and Olivia had first met the ultra-chic vampire film-maker on the set of *The Groves*, where she had been working as an assistant director. Ivy had spotted the romantic chemistry between Lillian and her father a mile away. Her dad hadn't been able to take his eyes off Lillian for a second when she had walked the red carpet at Olivia's big debut, and it didn't take super-powered vamp sight to see what that meant.

Lillian wrapped the twins in a double hug. 'I thought we'd all have dinner. Is that cool?'

'That's perfect!' Olivia clapped her hands, squealing. Ivy knew Olivia was beyond pleased that their father had fallen in love. Come to think of it, Olivia was beyond pleased when anyone fell in love. Ivy could only imagine what romantic scenes her sister anticipated taking place at her dance. *Yet another reason not to go.*

Lillian touched Olivia's elbow. 'How are you doing?' Her voice was soothing. 'Have you heard about the strike?'

So much for the dance distraction. Olivia wilted. 'Yes and it bites.'

'But look on the bright side. You now have a year to make sure you know the script backwards – and forwards, of course.'

'That's true.' Olivia stood up straighter, a smile

stretching across her lips. 'I hadn't thought of it that way.'

Ivy wasn't sure she was looking forward to a year of helping Olivia learn her lines. *The things I do for sisterly love!*

🦇   🦇   🦇

Ivy reached for a third helping of chocolate Marshmallow Platelets at the same time as Lillian. It was a favourite dessert for both of them and they were in a contest to see who could eat more.

'I give in!' Lillian laughed, letting her fork clatter to her plate. 'You are a force to be reckoned with, Ivy.'

'That she is,' said Charles, raising his crystal glass to his daughter.

Lillian folded her dark red napkin in a neat square on the table. Over dinner, Olivia had explained how she wouldn't be needed on set that summer.

'You're not the only one suffering as a result

of this whole writers' strike ordeal,' Lillian said, turning to Olivia. 'It's affected my job, too.'

'Is there a bright side for you?' Olivia asked.

'Well,' Lillian said, as her eyes flitted to Charles, 'I'll be staying in Franklin Grove until Hollywood reboots.'

Ivy and Olivia shared a mischievous look. No way could they let this opportunity slide.

'Ooooh!' Ivy teased her father. 'How romantic!'

'It's fate,' Olivia chimed. 'Just like that film where the couple have to share dinner because of a rainstorm. They think they hate each other, but really, they –'

'Love each other!' Ivy interrupted. 'Ah, true love. Isn't it the best?'

Ivy couldn't believe it, but her father was blushing. *Now I've seen everything!*

'Of course, I'm not one for anything too gushy, but I think it's totally cool that you two –'

Olivia dug an elbow into Ivy's ribs.

'Girls!' A smile threatened to crease the corners of Lillian's mouth. 'You need to quit teasing your dad.'

Olivia slapped her hand over her mouth, her blue eyes nearly bugging out of her head. 'Sorry,' she mumbled into her palm. 'Just kidding.'

Charles cleared his throat, recovering his typical suave composure. 'And I'll be getting my own back.'

Say what? Ivy didn't have a clue what her father meant.

'What's that supposed to mean?' Olivia's eyebrows pinched together.

'Oh, nothing.' Charles swished his hand through the air.

'Come on, Dad,' Ivy pressed. 'What do you mean?'

Charles smiled at his daughters. 'A father has to have a few secrets of his own, does he not?'

Ivy wished the answer was 'not'.

'Pass the Buttercup Yellow, please.'

Ivy tossed a bottle of nail polish to Olivia, who had just finished coating the nails on Ivy's right hand in a deep shade of Vampy Violet. Ivy blew on her fingernails. She had a bad habit of smudging them before they dried.

'So, what should we do for the holiday?' asked Ivy between puffs. 'Now that I won't be catching up on the latest episodes of *Shadowtown*, that is.'

'Good question.' Olivia brushed a layer of the bright yellow polish on to her toenails. 'I'm guessing you don't want to join Charlotte in her quest for the perfect tan?'

Ivy wrinkled her nose, studying the sheer white of her skin. 'I'm thinking no.'

'Right,' agreed Olivia.

'Maybe we could visit Aunt Rebecca on the farm, then?'

'Now *that* idea, I love.'

Aunt Rebecca was the only family they had on their mom's side – their mom's twin.

Thinking about her mom always made Ivy sad. She had been a non-vampire and their dad, with his Transylvanian vampire heritage, had risked everything to marry her. But she'd died during childbirth and Mr Vega had cut off all contact with the human side of the family, thinking it would be for the best. Ivy and Olivia had only recently found out about their aunt, but they'd already visited her several times. The outdoors didn't even make Ivy want to break out in hives any more. Plus, the horses had stopped running away every time she was around. Ivy was actually starting to love the place.

Olivia fanned her toes. 'I still don't know why it was so important for me to stay over tonight. Do you think it was because of the dinner with Lillian?'

'I don't think so. Dad probably would have

preferred us not to be around for that.' Ivy pulled open the lid of her coffin and climbed inside. It was a top-of-the-line Interna 3 and she loved the feel of the soft red velvet beneath her toes. Olivia pulled back her pink comforter and climbed into bed. She rested her head on the pillows with the pink lace trim and reached to adjust the ribbon that was tied in a big bow on the headboard. Her bed couldn't have been more different to Ivy's coffin.

'Then why tonight, of all nights?'

Ivy stretched her legs and snuggled into the cushioned velour. 'Maybe we'll find out in the morning.' *If I can sleep*, Ivy added in her head. *What on earth is my dad planning?*

Olivia yawned. Her ponytail was lopped sideways on top of her head and the sheets were tangled in a heap at her feet. There had been a noise at the door. Had she heard a knock?

Knock, knock!

There it was again. She peeked over the edge of her bed. Ivy's coffin was still sealed shut. Their bedroom door creaked open and Olivia heard the shuffle of feet as the edge of a brass tray came into view. A brass tray? The only serving options Olivia had seen at the Vegas' house were those cushioned trays used for TV dinners. She quickly tried to flatten her hair into something presentable.

The figure of a hulking man dressed in a full morning suit appeared in the open doorway. *It's Horatio!* Olivia thought, stunned. Horatio was her grandparents' butler. The Lazars were Transylvanian nobility. But what was he doing in Franklin Grove?

Olivia blinked. There was only one explanation. She had to be dreaming. Olivia pulled the sheets up to her chin and burrowed back beneath the covers.

41

A hand tapped Olivia's shoulder and her eyes snapped open. 'Madam?'

'Oh my goodness!' she shrieked.

The bulky Horatio leaped back and two glasses tipped over, spilling orange juice and blood-orange juice all over his neatly pressed suit.

'Oops.' Olivia's cheeks burned. 'I didn't mean to. I thought you were a dream.' She was about to ask Horatio what he was doing there when Ivy's coffin swung open, whacking poor Horatio so that he stumbled back into the wall behind him.

Ivy jolted out of her coffin like a vampire in a bad horror flick. 'What's going on?' She spotted the butler. 'What are you doing here?' Ivy rubbed her eyes with her fists.

Cautiously, Horatio placed the brass platter on the edge of Olivia's bed and handed Ivy a half-full glass of blood-orange juice and Olivia the remains of the regular orange juice.

'Thanks.' Olivia took a sip.

The butler rubbed the spot where he had been struck with Ivy's hard coffin-lid. 'Surprise!' he managed to choke out, like he'd been saving it up for the right moment. Olivia got the feeling that his breakfast treat had not gone as planned.

'Surprise!' Two more voices echoed from the doorway. Olivia almost spilled the orange juice again. There at Ivy's bedroom door were their grandparents, the Count and Countess Lazar.

'Oh my darkness,' exclaimed Ivy, clambering out of her coffin. 'What are you doing here?'

It was as if Transylvania had been transplanted directly into the Vega household. Olivia beamed. The Count and Countess swept into the room, and immediately Olivia felt underdressed in her polka-dotted flannel pyjamas. Her grandmother was wearing a black fitted corset top and a long, full skirt that dusted the floor as she floated along, arm-in-arm with their grandfather. The Count wore a crimson velvet jacket with ruffled sleeves peeking out of the cuffs of his blazer.

'We just flew in!' The Countess pulled Olivia into a tight hug. Now Olivia knew why it had been so important to have a sleepover last night. *My bio-dad is way too good at keeping secrets!* Olivia's heart swelled and she had the sudden desire to wrap her whole family into one, giant group hug.

'Tell me,' whispered the Count to Ivy. 'What is the pizza situation like here?'

Ivy winked. 'There's always plenty in the freezer just waiting to be heated,' she assured him. The Count liked to keep a stock of pizza handy.

Olivia noticed their dad, dressed in a quilted-satin dressing gown, looking on from behind his parents. 'So this is why I just *had* to sleep over!' she cried.

'Well, I could hardly let you miss out on a wake up like this.' He folded his arms, smiling.

Horatio, who had recovered his composure, stood stiffly off to the side. 'I would like to cordially invite you to the dining room.' He gestured for the family to follow and then led everyone in a line out of Ivy's bedroom.

In the dining room, the mahogany table had been covered by a fine silk tablecloth. Olivia's mouth watered at the yummy scents coming from a dozen platters. With a flourish, Horatio removed the sterling silver domes that covered the food.

'Bon appétit!' he said.

Olivia's eyes widened. A breakfast feast was laid out for the family, complete with blood sausage for the vampires and veggie sausage for Olivia. There were scones and buttered rolls and a mountain of scrambled eggs. Horatio had only been in the house for five minutes. Had he brought the food all the way from Transylvania?

'This looks deadly,' said Ivy, spooning a sausage patty on to her plate.

Olivia felt like she was getting the royal

treatment as Horatio draped a linen napkin over her lap. 'What brings you to Franklin Grove?' she asked her grandparents, stealing a scone for her plate.

'You girls, of course.' Grandma smacked her lips thoughtfully. 'We want to spend some time with you, doing . . . well, whatever you normally do.'

'Really?' Olivia had a hard time picturing her grandparents fitting into Franklin Grove life. In fact, she wasn't sure Franklin Grove was prepared for this level of old-school fabulous. 'Well, I was supposed to be doing an interview with my classmate, Charlotte, at Mister Smoothie.' Olivia hesitated. 'But it might not be the right sort of place for you.'

Olivia's bio-dad shuddered at the mere mention of the name 'Mister Smoothie'. She knew he was remembering the utter horror of being forced to dance to the Twist and Shout.

46

Grandpa crossed his knife and fork over his plate. 'I'm sure if it's somewhere you like, then we'll like it, too. Maybe we could all go there for a drink before you meet your friend,' he suggested.

Mr Vega shifted in his chair. 'It's not exactly a vamp establishment.'

'Oh, please!' the Countess hushed her son. 'We're five hundred years old. I think we can handle it.'

Ivy shrugged and Olivia knew they were both thinking the same thing. *This is going to be either hilarious . . . or horrible.*

Chapter Three

Mister Smoothie popped into view like an ominous raincloud – a brightly coloured, very musical raincloud, but a raincloud none the less. Ivy couldn't believe that she and Olivia were leading their father and grandparents to the least vampy place on earth. But at least her whole family was in one place. It hadn't been too long since it had just been Ivy and her father. Now, she was part of a big family. *I could definitely get used to this*, she thought.

A little girl on a tricycle passed them on the sidewalk, and her bright blue helmet swivelled as she stared at Ivy's grandparents. They looked better prepared to attend a gothic ball than take a stroll outside on the blistering asphalt. The girl stopped peddling, her jaw dropping open.

'Excuse me.' The little girl peered up at the Countess. 'But are you a queen?'

Ivy snorted. Her grandmother did look a bit – *ahem* – formal for an afternoon stroll.

Grandma chuckled. 'No,' she said, smoothing her dark velvet skirt. The fullness of it jutted out from her hips, making her appear majestic and grand. 'But you're awfully sweet to think so.' With a mischievous smile on her face, Countess Lazar dipped into a long, low curtsy, so graceful that Ivy would never have guessed her grandmother was more than five hundred years old! Even the Count looked surprised, and gave a hasty bow to join in.

🦇 🦇 🦇

The door chimed as the entire Lazar–Vega clan trooped into Mister Smoothie. Against the shop's bright pink and lime-green décor, Ivy's family stood out like flies in milk. A couple of patrons did double takes, probably because her grandparents and their butler looked like a fancy version of the Addams family. Nobody but the Count would wear a dark red suit in the middle of the afternoon and certainly no man in this decade would sport ruffles!

Ivy raised her hands in a human stop sign. 'How about we go ahead and order for everyone?' She didn't think her dignified grandparents were ready for a round of Mister Smoothie singing, or worse . . . dancing! Order the wrong smoothie and the staff at the shop would serenade the customer with peppy rock songs and choreographed dance numbers. The Count and Countess might have wanted to experience life at Franklin Grove, but Ivy wasn't sure they needed to experience it all at once.

While Charles and the Lazars went to save

them a table, Ivy and Olivia made a beeline for the counter, where machines were swirling with brightly coloured liquids.

'Which smoothie do you think is the most vampy?' Ivy asked, craning her neck to study the vibrant menu posted on the wall.

'I like Beauty-Boosting Blueberry,' Olivia suggested.

'Vampy?'

'Right, not so much. What about a Mocha Choca Latte? That's dark.' Olivia offered a lopsided smile. 'And you guys are, you know, kind of dark too.'

Ivy looked down at her combat boots and black pleated skirt and shrugged. 'Good a reason as any.' She waved to the girl in a bubblegum-pink apron behind the counter.

'Welcome to Mister Smoothie! We hope you're having a rock-'n'-rolling day!' The girl grinned at the twins.

Ivy could barely keep from 'rock-'n'-rolling' her eyes. 'We'll have one Mocha Choca Latte, please.' She turned to her sister. 'What else?'

Olivia muttered a few of the smoothie names under her breath as she read out from the menu, trying to decide what their grandparents might like. 'Oh, I know! Cherry-O!' exclaimed Olivia, exaggerating a British accent.

'What was *that*?'

'The smoothie name.' Olivia pointed. 'See? Like "Cheerio!" only it's *cherry*. Very English, don't you think? And,' she said, lowering her voice, 'the smoothie will be red, just like you-know-what.'

Ivy cocked her head. 'Like what?'

'Like, "I want to suck your bl—"' Olivia twirled her hand as if to encourage her sister to complete the sentence.

'It's not as simple as that!' Ivy swatted at her sister. 'We'll take two Tutti Fruttis and two

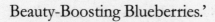

Beauty-Boosting Blueberries.'

Olivia started laughing. 'I never thought I'd hear you say "Tutti Frutti".'

Ivy gave a sly look sideways at her sister. 'Just don't tell anyone, OK?' *Especially not Brendan*, she almost added, but the last thing she needed was to give Olivia any ideas.

'Can you believe the Transylvanians are here in Franklin Grove, though?' Olivia glanced over her shoulder towards where their dad and grandparents were sitting erect in the vinyl booth. The Countess's eyes were wide as she took in the multicoloured surroundings. 'It's so . . . so . . .' Olivia searched for the word. 'It's fabulous!'

'It's also a little weird,' Ivy reminded her, just in case her sister was thinking of launching into a backflip, or worse – a cheer.

'That, too.' Olivia nodded. 'But I can't get over it. We have such a big family now. Can you believe

53

that we were both only-children our entire lives, and now *this*?'

'Hey!' Ivy put her fists on her hips. 'Did you pickpocket my brain? I was thinking the exact same thing only a minute ago.'

Olivia smiled. 'You know what would make our family gatherings even bigger?'

'What?' asked Ivy, watching the girl in the apron pour bright-red slush from a pitcher into a tall cup.

'Taking the whole family to Aunt Rebecca's farm! Then we'd really have everyone together.'

The cheerful waitress arranged five frosty glasses on a tray, which Ivy slid from the counter, being careful not to slosh the smoothies. 'And I thought *I* was the smart one,' said Ivy.

Olivia grabbed straws, while Ivy carried the smoothies back and handed them out to her family before slipping into the booth opposite her grandparents. *Thank goodness we managed to dodge the singing,* Ivy thought.

'It's . . . purple,' said the Countess, making whirlpools with her straw. Olivia giggled.

Ivy was about to tell her grandmother that the smoothie was *supposed* to be that colour, when a horrifying sound blasted into her super-vampire ears. Someone was ordering a Rock and Roller, and the song that went with it was at least ten times worse than the Twist and Shout.

Ivy did a quick calculation in her head. Could she get her family out of here in two seconds flat? She scanned the room. *No way.* The Lazars and Vegas would have to grit their vampire teeth and bear it. Here went nothing . . .

The waitresses and cashiers boogied out, snapping their fingers and getting the other patrons going.

'Rockin' around the shop tonight . . . Drinkin' cold smoothies . . . A chilly delight . . .'

The smoothie shop erupted into song, making

Ivy wish she could crawl back into her coffin. No such luck. Reluctantly, she swivelled to check on the Count and Countess, who were bound to be seriously offended. As far as she knew, her grandparents were still into music of the organ variety.

'Oh my darkness!' Ivy's mouth dropped. There were her grandparents, bopping away to the Rock and Roller song with Olivia. The Countess was even clapping.

'Bravo!' shouted the Count.

Ivy's father leaned closer. 'I guess you never know what will happen on a trip to Mister Smoothie.'

That's for sure, thought Ivy. The Count and Countess actually seemed disappointed when the song finished.

'So tell me,' said Ivy's grandmother, nestling back into the booth. 'How is school at Franklin Grove? What do they teach you there?'

Ivy thought this was an odd question, because Franklin Grove taught the same thing as any other school. 'You know, the usual stuff. We have Social Studies, Science, Algebra, Media Studies . . .'

Ivy's grandfather nodded along, as if her list of courses was fascinating. 'Interesting, interesting. Same for you, Olivia?'

'Yes, and this year I'm organising the school dance.' Olivia propped her cable-knit-clad elbows on the table. 'I've a mountain of work. We only found out about it yesterday and now I'm chairing the whole thing.'

Grandma's eyes brightened. 'You have great experience after attending the Transylvanian ball.' She winked, taking a sip from her purple concoction.

Several months before, Olivia and Ivy had travelled far across the Atlantic to meet their long-lost-family in Transylvania. The highlight of the trip had been an elegant vampire ball that even Transylvanian royalty had attended.

Olivia slurped her smoothie. 'I don't think it will be as fancy as that.' Ivy remembered how nervous Olivia had been about making her big debut into vampire society. She'd even worried about clashing with the crimson limousine décor!

Olivia's chirpy ringtone sounded from her purse. She fished it out, checked the screen and blushed. 'Sorry, but do you mind if I take this? It's Jackson.'

Ivy smiled. Olivia looked as if she had been poked with Cupid's arrow. How could anyone refuse that lovesick face?

The Countess waved Olivia on with ring-adorned hands, eyes crinkling at the corners.

'Thanks!' Olivia scooted out of the booth and scurried away from the group, phone pressed to her ear. 'Hiiiii . . .'

Ivy hoped she never sounded that mushy with

Brendan. She took another gulp of her smoothie.

'Isn't it sweet,' said the Count, watching Olivia. 'It's so nice to see a young girl who's found her destiny. Olivia wanted to be an actress and that's what she's become.'

Ivy frowned. Since when had the Count cared about Hollywood dreams? She couldn't remember him ever asking Olivia about her acting career or her romance with Jackson.

Grandma shifted in her seat. 'That's right!' she said brightly. 'Finding your right path in life is so important.' There seemed to be something forced about her smile as she watched Ivy closely.

Ivy looked from her grandma to her grandfather, and then across to her dad. He looked as if he'd swallowed a clove of garlic.

'What's going on?' Ivy asked. 'You guys look like you've been staked!'

The Count played with the ruffles of his sleeves, looking thoroughly uncomfortable.

'Now that we're alone,' he said, nodding towards Olivia, who was still chattering on the phone with Jackson, 'we'd like to have a quiet word with you, Ivy.'

'With me?' Ivy got a crawly feeling up the back of her neck. What could they need to tell her that Olivia wasn't meant to hear?

'There are some things you must know about being a growing vampire,' her grandfather continued. 'You see, when high-born vampires, like you, reach a certain age, their powers can become a bit – well – hard to manage. It can be time to learn to control your vampire skills. Become acquainted with your . . .' he gave a hard gulp, 'destiny.'

There's that word again, Ivy thought. *What are they trying to tell me?*

'Like when you hit Horatio with the coffin lid this morning,' the Countess pointed out.

Ivy winced. She hadn't meant to greet the day

quite so vigorously. She glanced over at Horatio, who was standing a short distance away, watching over the Lazars. His eyes followed the waitress as she wiped down tables, cleared cups and scooted chairs under tables – all Horatio's usual jobs. He looked positively twitchy. He could do these tasks at twice the pace. Just as Ivy was about to turn back, she noticed a plaster stuck to Horatio's temple. She shrank back in the booth. *Did I do that?* Then a worse thought occurred to her. Hitting Horatio was awful, but he was sturdy enough to handle the blow. *What if it had been Olivia that I'd hit with the coffin lid? I could have knocked her unconscious!*

'I didn't mean to!' Ivy pressed her hand to her chest. She was suddenly feeling panicky. She was a walking natural disaster! 'Are you sure there wasn't a defect in the coffin? Maybe we should check.'

'It's OK.' The Countess reached across the

table to hold Ivy's hand. 'There are ways to control your powers.'

'Like a pill?' she asked, envisioning herself as part of some freaky science experiment.

'No, nothing like that,' her grandmother reassured her. 'It's a school, actually. All Transylvanian vampires go to Wallachia Academy.'

Ivy had never heard of Wallachia. She couldn't even guess how to spell it.

'It's like a finishing school,' explained the Count. 'In fact, Wallachia is the premier place to learn to control powers and be a good vampire.'

Charles nodded. 'I studied there.' He straightened his shoulders, suddenly looking like a proud alumnus. Ivy was shocked. She had never known her dad had attended finishing school!

'And we met there.' Ivy's grandfather winked at the Countess and Ivy blushed. She had never seen her grandparents act so lovey-dovey in public! 'In fact,' the Count continued, 'everyone in the entire Lazar line has attended Wallachia. Oh, it's beautiful! Wrought-iron gates, towering castle spires, you'll love it!'

'I will?' asked Ivy, confused.

The Countess placed her hand on her husband's arm. 'We're getting ahead of ourselves. Ivy, we'd like it if you would come to Transylvania to study there, too.'

Ivy sat stunned. She knew she should say something and yet the only thought in her head was that she *didn't* have one thought in her head. She turned to look at Olivia. She'd been cornered by Charlotte, who'd just arrived, dressed head-to-toe in pink – pink cardigan, pink hair-ribbon and shiny pink lipgloss.

'Olivia!' Charlotte circled her interview subject, camera in hand. 'Can you tell us about the progress being made on the dance? Do we have a theme yet? What about a colour palette?' Charlotte asked the questions at rapid-fire speed.

Even though Olivia gave a swift eye roll, Ivy could still tell her sister was happy to be in front of the camera. Her face lit up, her posture straightened – Olivia was a total natural.

The Countess followed Ivy's stare. '*Who* is that girl with the orange skin?' she asked, pressing her hand over her mouth.

Ivy snickered. '*That* is Charlotte.'

Her grandmother squinted to peer closer. 'Oh my. Well, that certainly is an interesting look.'

Charlotte shuffled around Olivia to shoot a new angle. 'FYI, this is *so* your good side. Now, give me a look that says, "I'm overworked."'

The corners of Olivia mouth curved down and she scrunched her face. 'Huh?'

'That's perfect!' Charlotte took a step back, knocking over a glass with her elbow. Ivy spotted a blur of motion and the corner of a tablecloth whipping up. It was Horatio. Like a superhero, he lunged for the smoothie cup that had been knocked from the table, catching it in a split second. His reflexes had been so fast, not one of the bunnies had even seen him in action. But there he was, adjusting the glass like he'd been there all along. Ivy looked on, amazed. So maybe there *were* advantages to honing her powers.

Ivy returned her attention to her grandparents, noticing that the Count had nearly drained his Tutti Frutti smoothie already. 'So it's like vamp summer school?' she asked.

The Countess pursed her lips, sharing a look with Ivy's grandfather. 'Well . . . you may have to attend a bit longer than that. The teachers give their assessment only after an initial appraisal.'

'Longer? Longer than a summer?' Ivy chewed her lip, thankful her fangs were filed. She wished this conversation wasn't happening behind

Olivia's back. This had come as such a surprise; she was badly in need of some sister-support. All this talk was stressing her out. Ivy could actually feel her blood pressure spike. She slid her smoothie closer and took another long sip. Every muscle in her body was tense. Her hands tightened around her glass and then – *crack!* – it shattered, and bright red smoothie flooded the table like molten lava from a volcano.

'Oops.' Ivy's cheeks felt warm. 'Maybe I do have a bit of that super-strength.' She tried to scoop the broken glass into a pile, but it was no use. There was smoothie everywhere!

Ivy's dad chuckled. 'A bit?'

Thankfully, Horatio appeared with a small bottle of Spray and Shine and began wiping up Ivy's mess. 'Not to worry, Miss Ivy. I can take care of this straight away.'

Where does he keep that thing? Ivy wondered. In a flash, the table was spotless. Meanwhile, Olivia had finished her interview with Charlotte and was walking over to rejoin the family.

To Ivy's surprise, though, her grandparents looked alarmed. 'Ivy, listen.' Her grandmother leaned over the table. 'You can't tell your sister about Wallachia Academy under any circumstances.' She glanced quickly in Olivia's direction. 'It's one of the greatest vampire academies. Non-vampires can never know about it.' The Countess looked seriously grave over this last point.

'But she's my sister!' Ivy wanted to remind them that bunnies weren't supposed to know about vampires at all, but Olivia did and *that* had worked out perfectly.

The Lazars shook their heads. Even Ivy's father whispered, 'Your grandparents are right, Ivy. We need to keep this conversation private.' How could he agree with them? He had broken the First Law of the Night with her mother as well. She started to protest, but a quick shake of his head stopped her.

Olivia slid into the booth next to Ivy, retrieving her barely touched smoothie. 'Um . . .' She looked from face to face. 'Did I miss something?' Olivia slurped her purple concoction. 'You look like you all just got back from the morgue.'

Olivia had hit the nail in the coffin. That was exactly how Ivy felt.

The Countess, however, rushed to explain. 'No, no, Olivia, we were just chatting about how different things are here. Much more . . .'

'. . . enthusiastic,' the Count finished off her sentence.

'Oh,' said Olivia. She flattened her cheek into her palm and stared off into space. 'Yeah, really different.'

'OK,' said Ivy, poking her sister. '*Now* who looks like they've just got back from the morgue?'

Olivia's shoulders sagged. 'I'm going to tell you something.' Olivia squeezed Ivy's leg. 'But you can't laugh.'

'Cross my heart,' Ivy promised, trying to guess at what Olivia could have to say. She checked to make sure the adults at the table were happily occupied in conversation.

Olivia took a deep breath. 'Jackson fell asleep on the phone with me.'

Ivy almost spewed a mouthful of smoothie on to Olivia's lap. 'He what?'

'He actually fell asleep!' She dropped her head into her hand. 'He was in Hawaii and it was like five o'clock in the morning.'

Ivy glanced to make sure the adults were still talking amongst themselves. 'Wait, why did he call if it was five o'clock in the morning?'

Olivia didn't meet her sister's eye. 'I may have texted and said I had something important to tell him.'

'And . . .' Ivy prodded, trying to piece together her sister's story.

'And that he simply had to call me.' Olivia scrunched her shoulders up to her ears.

'Well, what was it?'

Olivia was almost as pink as her sweater. 'Um, that I miss him.'

Ivy cracked up and pulled her sister into a hug. Ivy wished *she* could text Olivia that there was something big to tell *her*. Something like: *There's a vampire academy in Transylvania and I might have to go to it.* Ivy glanced at her father, who was busy explaining the menu to the Lazars. She hated keeping secrets from Olivia. The thought of it made her stomach twist like a handful of curly fries, but she couldn't say anything. Not yet anyway.

Two waitresses walked by with rags and bottles of Spray and Shine. 'I think I'm going crazy,' said the waitress in the bubblegum-pink apron. 'Two of the tables in my section have been cleared and I can't for the life of me remember doing them.'

Ivy fought back the urge to laugh. Horatio had been hard at work again.

Chapter Four

Olivia's heartbeat had been steadily increasing the nearer the car got to school. As her adoptive dad, Mr Abbott, edged the wheels to the curb, Olivia teetered dangerously close to full freak-out mode.

'But, Dad,' she said, unbuckling her seatbelt, 'how can I possibly organise a school dance that will please everyone?' Olivia had been racking her brain ever since she took on the job as chairperson, and yet she hadn't come up with one theme idea that would please both the goths and the bunnies.

Mr Abbott put his hand on his daughter's

shoulder. 'Olivia, a wise man makes his own decisions; an ignorant man follows public opinion. Make your own decisions and I know you will do wonderfully.'

Olivia gave her dad a weak smile. She always appreciated his Zen advice, but sometimes she thought it might be better suited to yoga class than to real life. She climbed out and waved goodbye, smoothing her lilac minidress as Mr Abbott's car disappeared around a corner.

Olivia hesitated in front of Franklin Grove School, suddenly struck with the memory of her *old* school, where she'd been studying before moving here – before she even knew she had a twin. The modern school building had looked like a box, painted a combination of ugly beige and dirt-brown. Franklin Grove was ancient in comparison. Leafy vines draped from the huge columns that framed the entrance and a heavy oak front door led into a yawning hallway. Olivia smiled, recalling her first day here. She had been terrified that she would stay the friendless new girl forever. *But look at me now – I'm head of the biggest event at this school!* She could do this.

With one more shaky breath, she stepped inside for her first school-dance committee meeting.

'Right on time, Miss Chairperson,' Jenny greeted Olivia cheerfully at the door to the school common room. The janitor had been kind enough to open it for use over the weekend and Olivia felt like a businesswoman conducting a meeting in some fancy corporate conference room. If fancy corporate conference rooms came decorated with spirit week posters.

Jenny opened the door for Olivia. 'So, um . . . how is the planning coming?' She raised her eyebrows, looking hopeful.

'I guess we'll find out,' Olivia said, smiling.

'So, what are you wearing to the dance?' Jenny

asked, keeping pace alongside Olivia as she made her way around the room, trying to figure out the best place to set up for the meeting.

'I haven't even had time to think about it! But I can't be the worst dressed when I'm chairing the whole dance!'

'Don't worry,' Jenny replied quickly. 'You've still got plenty of time. I'm sure you'll find something that Jackson Caulfield will totally love.'

'If he can come,' Olivia murmured.

Inside the common room, three girls from the grade above Olivia had taken a huddle of comfy seats. Olivia thought she recognised them from the cafeteria. *That's odd. I didn't think people from the grades above us got involved with the committee.* She pulled her shoulders back and strode up to the front of the room. The girl in the middle of the three stood up, extending a hand to Olivia.

'Well, hello . . . Olivia, is it?' The girl wore a pair of cropped white jeans, to-die-for wedges, and a bright yellow halter top that matched her long ponytail. 'I wanted to introduce myself. I'm Lucrezia. And this is Melinda and Veronica.'

'Nice to meet –' Olivia started.

'But don't worry about learning our names. You can just call each of us "Boss".'

Boss? A worm of anxiety burrowed into Olivia's stomach. She glanced over at Jenny for support, but her eyes were glued to the floor. Was this why she had been so eager to give up her position? Other committee members were walking into the room now, settling into seats.

'It's so nice of you to join us.' Olivia put on a big smile.

'You two can go ahead and show yourselves to your seats.' Lucrezia's tone was sickly-sweet. Olivia looked around, but now that the other committee members had arrived, there was only a pair of hard wooden stools standing isolated in the corner. 'Those will do.' Lucrezia had noticed Olivia looking at the stools.

Jenny went obediently over to one of the empty stools. But Olivia didn't budge.

'Let's cut to the chase.' Lucrezia twirled a strand of her ponytail around one finger. '*We're* in charge of this dance, no matter who's officially on the committee, got it? We ran it last year and we're going to do the exact same thing this year. We just want to make sure everyone's on the same page. Are we?'

Perched sadly on her stool, Jenny looked like a moulting parakeet. Was Olivia really going to join her? Then she remembered her dad's cryptic Zen advice: 'A wise man makes his own decisions; an ignorant man follows public opinion.'

'Excuse me,' Olivia piped up, smiling her brightest smile. 'I think there must be some confusion. Girls in my grade organise the dance, so, if you don't mind scooting over, I can get to organising.'

Melinda – or was it Veronica? – jumped out of her chair and looked ready to say something, when she froze. Olivia traced her gaze to the back of the room. The door was swinging shut behind Charlotte, and she had a camera on her shoulder.

'Sorry,' Charlotte mouthed, and then her loud voice cut the tense atmosphere. 'Pretend I'm not here. Act natural!'

When Olivia turned back, Melinda, Lucrezia and Veronica were acting anything but natural. All three had bright smiles plastered across their lips. Clearly, none of them wanted to be caught on camera acting like total bullies. *Which is exactly what they are*, Olivia reminded herself. *No way are they pushing me around!*

Lucrezia patted Olivia on the back. 'How silly of us to forget that it was your grade in charge of the dance.' She levelled her stare, meeting Olivia's eyes. 'Please call us if you need any help.'

To Olivia's relief, the girls traipsed out one

after the other. Jenny watched them depart, then cast Olivia an apologetic glance.

'I'm sorry,' she said, standing up off the stool. 'Those girls . . .'

Olivia cleared her throat and rolled her eyes towards the camera that Charlotte still had trained on them.

'I know!' she said in a bright voice. 'They're so kind to offer to help.'

A shiver ran down Olivia's spine. *Of course. Those girls don't want to look mean in front of the camera! But how long will Charlotte's filming be able to hold them off?* Olivia's guess was not long, because at the doorway Melinda span on her heel and shot her a look so nasty it made her want to take a bath.

'Yikes,' Jenny muttered under her breath. 'Well . . . I knew I chose the right chairperson.'

Olivia wasn't so sure. She'd started feeling a little woozy. She may have won this battle, but she definitely had not won the war.

'Hey, Olivia!' Charlotte beckoned her over. 'Want to get a sneak peek of our interview from the other day?'

'Absolutely!' Olivia said, feeling her enthusiasm come back. This was supposed to be fun, and she wasn't going to let three wannabe pageant-queens on a power trip ruin that.

Charlotte flipped open the screen on the side of the camera and the interview loaded. Olivia watched, nervously. To her relief, she was pleased with her answers, and she didn't look like a total dork on camera, even without a crew of stylists and make-up artists behind her. She must have gained more than a hot celebrity boyfriend on set after all! Learning poise and a little screen presence were added perks!

Just as she was about to compliment Charlotte on her filming skills, she spotted Ivy in the background of the scene. Her sister's hand was squeezing around a super-thick Mister Smoothie glass and, then . . . *pow*! It shattered in a big oozing mess. That had to be vampire super-strength! No normal girl could break a glass with her bare hands. Olivia could hardly squeeze an aluminium can. Why hadn't she noticed the commotion back in the café? No way could she let this stay on camera – everyone would find out about her sister's secret vampire skills and her vamp family would be exposed.

Olivia eyed Charlotte carefully, trying to judge whether she had noticed Ivy's show of super-strength. Charlotte's face lit up every time she heard her own voice come through the audio, which, for once, was perfectly OK with Olivia. Charlotte was so focused on *Charlotte* that she hadn't seemed to notice Ivy in the background. Still, Olivia was going to have to do something about this.

'You think I could take a look at your camera?'

asked Olivia. It would only take her a second to go through the footage and delete the scene.

'Sure. It's the best my dad could buy,' Charlotte said, beaming. She shifted the camera into Olivia's hands but, as soon as she got hold of it, Olivia heard a beeping noise. A red light on the side of the camera flashed and the screen flickered to blank. Olivia shook the camera, hoping it would come back to life like a zombie from the dead.

'Hey, be careful!' Charlotte protested. 'Do you know how much this thing cost?' She snatched the camera back. It must have been out of batteries. *How utterly great.* Olivia had lost her chance. Now she would have to find another way to delete the interview before anyone saw it.

Charlotte squinted at the blank camera screen.

'This sucks,' she said, fiddling with the battery compartment. 'I was hoping to get some behind-the-scenes footage and I may not make any of the other committee meetings – I'll be super-busy planning my outfit.'

'That is a shame,' Olivia said. She meant it, too. It seemed as if that camera was the only thing that could fend off the Mean Musketeers. In the meantime, she still had a committee meeting to manage . . .

🦇   🦇   🦇

'How about a marshmallow tier-cake?' one person suggested, raising a hand in the air.

'What about a balloon arch for people to walk under as they arrive?' a girl at the back of the hall called out.

'I know a great DJ!' one boy offered.

Olivia scribbled down the suggestions using her pink fuzzy-topped pen. Fabulous ideas were flying from all directions. This dance had the potential to be a knockout success!

The door wheezed open, and Olivia glanced up. It was the trio – Lucrezia, Melinda and

Veronica. It was at times like these when Olivia would have really appreciated Jackson's security entourage.

One of the girls leaned over Charlotte and asked, 'Is that thing working?'

Charlotte raised her eyebrows, surprised to be addressed. 'Um, no, sorry. The battery's dead.'

The girls sent razor-sharp smiles in Olivia's direction. 'No problem,' Veronica said in a loud voice. 'No problem at all.' They strutted down the room on their colourful espadrilles and chunky wedges. 'Miss us?' she asked.

Not really, Olivia wanted to say. *What are* they *doing back?*

'We came up with a few ideas of our own. All we want to do is help.' She looked around the room and it was like an ice storm passing over everyone's heads. 'Like here's one: I think we should ban all goths and nerds from this dance. Everyone who's with me say, "Aye!"'

'Aye!' Lucrezia and Melinda raised their hands before anyone had a chance to protest.

Talk about a hostile takeover, thought Olivia. She squared her shoulders and took a giant step forwards.

'Ahem,' Olivia cleared her throat.

Melinda whipped around. 'Can it, you cheerleading cloudhead.'

Olivia's mouth dropped open and there was a collective gasp from the room. *She did not just say that!* Olivia sank into a chair. She had completely lost her ability to speak.

'Aren't you going to do something?' Charlotte mumbled from the seat beside her. 'No way would I let someone speak to me like that.' Olivia knew their behaviour had to be bad when even Charlotte was alarmed. For a moment, she wished Ivy was with her. *Ivy would know what to do. She always knows what to do.*

But what was Olivia going to do? The dance

was in jeopardy before it had even begun, the secret of her twin's vampire super-strength was in danger of being exposed and three mega-divas were muscling in on her action. And that wasn't even taking into account the fact that her boyfriend was hundreds of miles away and unlikely to be giving her a hug any time soon.

She watched the three bullies flicking their ponytails over their shoulders as they smirked at each other. Olivia let out a big sigh.

How much can one girl take?

Chapter Five

Ivy could get used to having Horatio around. It wasn't every day that you enjoyed a three-course lunch chock-full of meaty goodness in the Vega household. It was only noon and she was already stuffed! Too bad Olivia had been busy with her committee meeting and hadn't been able to join them.

Ivy's grandmother dabbed at the corners of her mouth with a black cloth napkin. 'Well, darling. Have you put any more thought into Wallachia Academy?' An emerald necklace glittered at the Countess's neck, casting green prisms of light on the dining-room table.

No. In fact, Ivy had been trying her best to avoid the subject completely. 'Not really,' she confessed. The thought of leaving Franklin Grove behind was almost too much to bear. But, on the other hand, so was the thought of disappointing her grandparents.

The Countess folded her hand over the Count's. 'We really think it would be for the best.'

'And that you would grow to love it. Did we mention it's in a big Gothic castle? With flying buttresses and beautiful stone gargoyles and spindly towers,' Ivy's grandfather added. He had traded his crimson coat for a sleek black tuxedo jacket. 'And you should see the kitchens!' He winked at Ivy, and she knew he was thinking about all the pizza she could eat there.

'Oh, yes! And the professors are top-notch. Nowhere in the world is there such a robust curriculum for young vampires.' Ivy thought maybe her grandmother ought to do a second stint there if she was so excited about it.

'All in a school?' she asked, pushing the leftover meat around on her plate.

The Countess's eyes sparkled. 'That's what we've been trying to tell you. Wallachia Academy is not just any old school. It is the best vampire academy in the world. It was founded by Vladimir Ivanov, the longest-living vampire of all time, and it has produced some of the finest vampire thespians, artists and Nobel laureates. Every generation of the Lazar family has attended – even your father did. Going there, you will learn all sorts of new vampire skills. Plus, you'll learn to control your powers. What could be better?'

Ivy sighed. 'I get that you want me to attend, but I don't know if Wallachia Academy is the right place for me.'

'Of course, we understand you don't want to leave your friends behind, or Olivia. We'd never ask you to do anything that would make you truly unhappy, but we honestly believe this is the best thing for you. We're sure you'd thank us one day,' said the Countess. 'We promise.'

Ivy's pulse quickened. 'I don't know how, when I can't even tell my sister where I'm going!'

'This isn't just about us, Ivy.' Her grandfather pushed back from the table. 'These vampire secrets have to be respected. Which is another important thing you'll learn at Wallachia Academy.'

'For your information, sharing the vampire secret with Olivia was one of the best things I've ever done. Can't you see that not all secrets are worth keeping?' Ivy knew her voice was getting so loud that she was almost shouting, but she couldn't help it. It looked as if her grandparents might spontaneously combust, their faces were so pink.

The Count's voice was steady when he finally spoke. 'Ivy, you're not appreciating how important your vampire heritage is to all of us.

If it wasn't, we wouldn't have travelled halfway around the world to talk to you – and at our age, too.'

Ivy felt like she'd been stabbed through with an iron stake. 'I'm sorry if you left Transylvania because of me, but . . . but . . .' Ivy couldn't finish her sentence. She was too close to tears. 'I'm sorry,' she managed to say at last. 'I need to be alone right now.' Then she sprinted to her room, squeezing past Horatio, who stood by the doorway with his gloved hands folded in front of him. Her father called after her, but she didn't stop. She couldn't. The only person she wanted to talk to was Brendan. She grabbed her cell phone from her nightstand and slammed the door to her bedroom. *Since when did I become the drama queen?*

She slid open her window, hiked one leg over the sill and climbed down the trellis out into the backyard. She hoped the fresh air would help clear her head. Then she dialled Brendan's number and took a seat on the rough brick of the Vegas' backyard patio. Out here, she didn't feel so trapped.

Brendan picked up. 'Ivy?' He sounded concerned, and she imagined his dark eyebrows puckered. 'I thought you were supposed to be having lunch with your grandparents today.'

'I was.' Ivy rested her chin on her knees. 'I mean, I did.'

'That was quick.'

'Brendan, it was a disaster! They want me to go to finishing school in Transylvania, some place called Wallachia Academy. It's supposed to be the most A-positive place on earth, but I already can't stand it. I'd have to leave you and Olivia. Plus, they won't let me tell Olivia and I actually yelled at my grandparents. Can you believe it?' Ivy was glad Brendan wasn't here in person. She felt like she might burst into tears at any moment, and she didn't want him to see her looking like a gothic clown when her eyeliner started to run.

There was silence on the other end of the phone, and then he said, 'I'm sure your family are doing what they think is right.' His voice was gentle. 'Although . . .' Ivy heard him take a deep sigh, 'I don't want you to go to some school across an entire ocean either.'

'I know! I'd rather go to the school dance than leave my home behind.' She laughed at how silly that idea was. *Me! In a frilly dress at a school dance!* The line went silent. Ivy waited. 'Hello? Brendan, are you still there?' She held the receiver away from her ear, quickly checking the screen. 'Brendan?'

'I'm here.' Brendan sounded like he had swallowed soda the wrong way. 'I think the school dance might be fun if we went together. You know?'

Ivy wasn't sure what to say. *Fun?* Was Brendan

kidding with her? 'Yeah, right!' she said, laughing. Then Ivy heard the door behind her open. She turned to see her dad stepping outside. 'Hey, Brendan? My dad's here. I've got to run.' She ended the call and prepared herself for a nice long father–daughter lecture. *How absolutely fatal,* she thought.

Charles sat down next to Ivy. He was still wearing his velvet smoking jacket, and the expression on his face was grim. Ivy was seriously considering digging her own grave.

'Your grandparents only want to do the right thing.' Her father's voice was immediately soothing. 'You don't have to make a decision yet. Why don't you sleep on it?'

Ivy swallowed hard. Maybe she had over-reacted . . . just a bit. The two of them sat in silence for several moments.

'I guess I should apologise to them,' she said eventually.

Her dad smiled and put an arm around her shoulders. 'They're old and they've travelled a long way,' he reminded her. 'We need to make allowances if they're a bit . . . to the point. It's only because they care.'

The two of them got to their feet and made their way back inside.

The Count and Countess were sitting stiffly on the edge of the couch. Ivy could barely meet their glance, she was so mortified.

'I'm sorry for running out of the room.' Ivy had worms crawling in her stomach. She felt dreadful. Never in twelve centuries would she have guessed she'd ever get into a fight with her sweet grandparents.

There was nothing else for it – she went and wrapped both of them in tight hugs.

When she pulled away, her grandfather was wringing his hands. 'I can't believe we upset you so. It was silly to mention our age. We would

95

have come to Franklin Grove anyway. We love travelling!'

'Yes, yes,' the Countess rushed to agree. 'We're happy to be here visiting you and Olivia. But surely you can understand. We would dearly love to see our granddaughter become the very best vampire she can possibly be.'

'I understand.' Ivy could see her grandparents believed in what they were saying and weren't just trying to make her toe the vampire line. 'But I still don't think Wallachia Academy will be right for me.' She couldn't just take off and leave her sister with no explanation.

The Countess pressed her wrinkled lips into a thin line, nodding. 'Very well. At least we tried.' Like most vampires, Ivy's grandmother had different-coloured eyes – one green, the other a rich amber – and both looked close to tears.

Ivy hated disappointing them, but she had other loyalties as well. Like her loyalty to Olivia.

'I promise,' said Ivy, 'I will always try to be the best vampire I can be.'

Her grandmother pulled Ivy into another hug. 'Oh, Ivy, I know that is true!'

A loud sniffle came from the corner of the room. When Ivy turned round, Horatio was wiping a tear from the corner of his eye.

❤ ❤ ❤

'I'm surprised the dance committee can survive without their fearless leader for one day,' said Ivy, tossing a pillow at her sister. 'What have you left them doing?'

Olivia was sprawled on the bed in Ivy's room, sucking on a Cherrylicious lollipop. She propped herself up on her elbows. She wasn't so sure the committee *could* survive without her, but tomorrow she and Ivy were going to Aunt Rebecca's farm, and that meant another twin sleepover at the Vegas' house. Olivia had written detailed instructions for Jenny. 'Follow these and you'll be fine,' she'd told her:

Take suggestions for a theme
Make a list of supplies
Check the budget
And most importantly, try not to let Lucrezia,
Melinda and Veronica boss you around. I know it's
hard, but try!

A mental image of Jenny, with her mousy-brown hair and her shoulders hunched over, snapped into Olivia's mind. 'Maybe I'd better call to check in with Jenny. They're supposed to be thinking about themes, but . . . you know. Just in case.' Olivia fumbled inside her straw tote bag for her phone. 'Hi, Jenny?' she said when Jenny picked up. 'I was just calling to double-check that you all don't mind having a committee meeting without me . . .' She held her breath.

'Honestly?' Jenny's voice was high-pitched.

'I'm not so sure.'

Not so sure, thought Olivia, trying to stifle a groan. She had cleared this with everyone yesterday.

'It's just, well, what about Lucrezia and her friends?' Jenny continued. 'I don't know if I can keep them in line.'

Unfortunately, Jenny was right. Those girls would stomp her like a chewed stick of spearmint under their platform heels.

Olivia twisted one of her bangle bracelets around her wrist, until suddenly she had an idea. 'Jenny, leave those girls to me. I'll call you later with an update.' She snapped the phone shut.

'You *are* going stand up to those girls, right?' said Ivy, jabbing a chopstick into her dark bun. Olivia had told her twin all about their performance at the first committee meeting.

The thought of confrontation made Olivia queasy, but she couldn't just leave Jenny to become roadkill. 'What's the one thing bullies can't handle?' Olivia asked, more to herself than to Ivy.

'I don't know. Teachers hanging around?'

Not a bad suggestion, thought Olivia, but that wasn't what she was getting at. 'Bullies can't stand it when the victims push back. What I need to learn is how to push!'

'Care to borrow a bit of my super-strength?' asked Ivy.

'Hopefully, I'll just need my brains this time!' Olivia jumped off the bed and skipped down the stairs to the living room, where Mr Vega was lounging on the couch with an open newspaper.

'Dad? I was wondering: do Ivy and I have time to slip out before dinner?'

Ivy pulled up behind her. She gave Olivia a confused look, but played along.

Olivia's bio-dad agreed. 'I guess,' he said, folding his paper. 'How much trouble could you get into before dinner?' *Quite a bit*, thought Olivia. Especially if she was armed with a few dollars.

'Where are we going?' Ivy asked, as they grabbed their jackets and headed out of the front door.

Olivia grinned. 'To the mall!'

Ten minutes later, Olivia and Ivy were power-walking through the busy shoppers and the strong smell of food-court pretzels. They passed Pink and Pretty, Dancing Delight, Trudy's Beauty Palace . . . *If I weren't here strictly on business, the temptation of all this shopping would be too much to resist!* Olivia thought.

'How are you going to find them here?' Ivy asked, trotting alongside Olivia. 'I mean, I assume this is about those three dance-committee bullies.'

'Trust me,' said Olivia, 'I'll find them.' But the closer she got to her destination, the more uncertain she felt. What if she couldn't reason with the girls? What if she forgot what to say?

With balled fists, she marched into Panzers department store, where, sure enough, the three older girls were right where Olivia had suspected – the make-up counter. Lucrezia sat in one of the tall black make-up chairs while Melinda added bright pink-coloured streaks to her friend's long blonde hair. Veronica was leaning close to a mirror, admiring the thick, shimmery blush she had painted over her cheekbones.

'Fashion victim alert,' Ivy whispered. Olivia agreed. Apparently these girls had never heard the phrase, 'too much of a good thing'.

She tugged Ivy into the shoe department and ducked behind a display of knee-high riding boots. 'What now?' asked Olivia.

Ivy blinked. 'I thought you had a plan?'

Olivia bit the side of her thumb. 'I do. I'm just . . . bracing myself.'

'Well, consider yourself braced!' Ivy's eyes grew wide. 'You *have* to go over there.'

'OK, OK, I'm going!' Olivia took a deep breath. She had once balanced one-legged on top of a cheerleading pyramid in front an entire football stadium. *Compared to that, how hard can this be?* She walked over to the girls. 'Lucrezia, Melinda, Veronica, I've had enough of you muscling in on the school dance.' Olivia tried to keep her voice from quaking. 'It's not right and it's not fair.' Channelling her sister, Olivia put her hands on her hips and waited.

The trio glanced around at one another and then Lucrezia burst into a fit of laughter. She doubled over, grabbing her stomach. Evidently, Olivia was quite the comedian.

Melinda stood over Olivia, at least four inches taller. 'Who do you think you are, talking to us like that?' Olivia was seriously regretting her choice of ballet flats. 'You're *younger* than us!' This was enough to send Lucrezia and Veronica into hysterics.

Olivia's face blazed. She was starting to back away, when she remembered how she'd managed to deal with Jessica Phelps when the actress had tried to humiliate her at the Hollywood awards. She thought about sending the girls her best killer death stare, but then something made her stop. *Don't stoop to their level.*

'I just want you to know that if you interfere with the committee again, you'll leave me no choice but to formally ask for you to be banned from meetings. I'm sure none of us wants that. It wouldn't look good on your school records.' Olivia narrowed her eyes to let them know she meant business. 'If I were you, I wouldn't push your luck.'

She'd kept her voice pleasant, but there was no mistaking how serious Olivia was.

Veronica flipped her hair over her shoulder. 'Fine. We'll stay away . . . or whatever.'

Olivia arched an eyebrow, silently congratulating herself on her acting skills. 'That's better.'

Then, without waiting for a response, she pivoted on the spot and walked over to Ivy.

The two of them breezed out of the store. When they'd got round the corner, Olivia pulled out her phone and busied herself dialling Jenny's number.

'Hello, Jenny? No need to worry. You'll be fine to go ahead without me for one meeting.' Olivia grinned at her sister. 'I guarantee it.' She hung up and skipped next to Ivy.

'You were impressive back there,' Ivy told her. 'Cold as ice. You should be a vampire!'

'Yeah, go to vampire school or something!' Olivia joked. Ivy slowed to a stop and watched her twin pull ahead.

You have no idea how close to the truth you are, Ivy thought. *One of us really* might *be about to enrol at a vampire academy.*

🦇　　　🦇　　　🦇

When Ivy and Olivia returned home, they found

their father pacing in the hallway. Olivia had told him they were going to the mall. He didn't need to be worried. She checked her watch. They weren't late. Was something wrong?

'Dad?' Ivy tapped him on the shoulder. 'We're home.'

'Great.' He flashed a smile. 'How does my hair look?'

What?

Olivia examined his dark, slicked-back hair. He always looked old-world dashing. 'Like it always looks?' she said, shrugging.

Mr Vega shook his head, as if trying to bring himself back to reality. 'Right, of course. Girls, your grandparents are in the dining room. We're about ready to eat.'

'Aren't you coming?' Olivia asked, but her bio-dad had stopped paying attention because, at that instant, the doorbell rang. 'I'll get it.' Olivia scurried over to the door. She didn't know they were expecting guests.

On the other side of the threshold stood Lillian, looking a little more prim than usual. She wore a black pencil skirt and matching cardigan, with a deep purple silk scarf tied around her neck. 'Wow,' said Olivia, breathless. 'You look fabulous!' She welcomed Lillian inside. 'What's the occasion?' Then she understood. The Lazars were here – her bio-dad's parents – and Lillian had never met them. Olivia let out an excited squeal. Lillian was meeting the parents!

The Lazars appeared from the dining room to stand beside Charles. Olivia took Lillian's purse, thinking that perhaps Lillian looked a bit shakier than usual as she entered the Vega household.

'Hello, Countess Lazar.' Lillian curtseyed. 'Nice to meet you, Count Lazar.' She gave a second curtsy. She was doing all the right things. Even Ivy looked pleased. But Lillian wasn't done.

'I have something for you.' For the finishing touch, Lillian pulled out a beautiful gold frame from her purse. The Countess gasped and Olivia and Ivy hurried to see what Lillian had given their grandparents. Inside the frame was a picture of Ivy, Olivia, and their father, Charles, dressed up in their red-carpet best for the *Bright Stars* awards show.

'It's perfect!' their grandmother exclaimed, reaching to give Lillian a hug.

Mr Vega kissed Lillian on the cheek and took her hand.

The Countess cupped her hand around her mouth as if telling Lillian a secret, but she didn't lower her volume. 'My son has always had excellent taste in companions.'

Olivia and Ivy shared a glance. That was great news for Lillian. But did it also mean their grandmother was beginning to accept that their dad had been right to marry their mother?

Olivia stretched out on top of the purple comforter in Ivy's bedroom, resting her hand on her full belly. 'Don't get me wrong,' she said. 'I love having our grandparents here, but if Horatio keeps making his three-course feasts for every meal, I'm going to float away like a blimp!'

'No kidding.'

The twins had left the grown-ups downstairs, flipping through an old photo album. They loved their father, but they didn't need to see any more of his baby pictures. That was something only a girlfriend could enjoy.

Ivy took a seat on her closed coffin and fired up her laptop.

Olivia turned on her side, bending a pillow in half to prop up her head. 'Ivy? I'm worried about Jackson.'

Ivy hardly glanced up.

'It's just that I keep trying to catch up with

him, but he's always busy or sleepy – stupid time differences. The last time I had a real conversation with him . . . well . . .' Olivia felt the familiar knot form in her stomach. 'I heard a knock at the door and someone came in saying, "A dozen red roses for Mr Jackson Caulfield."'

'What?' Ivy was typing furiously on her keyboard.

'Come on!' Olivia tossed her pillow at Ivy. 'You're not even listening.'

'Huh?' Ivy looked up briefly from the screen.

Olivia eyed her sister. Ivy had tilted the screen so that Olivia couldn't see what was on it. Come to think of it, that was exactly what Olivia did when she was online-shopping.

'Hey! Are you on the VVV?' The World Vide Veb was the vampire version of the Internet. Olivia jumped up to sit next to her sister. 'I want to look!' If there was shopping to be done, Olivia wanted to join in.

But as soon as she sat down, Ivy hit the sleep button on the computer and the screen went blank. She flipped the laptop closed and pushed it underneath her pillow. 'I'm all ears!' Ivy told Olivia. She pulled the sides of her ears out from her head. 'Plus, they're super vampy ears, so I can listen extra well!'

Olivia gave a one note laugh. *What can Ivy have been looking at online? She never puts her laptop underneath her pillow.*

'Fine.' Olivia didn't feel like obsessing about Jackson any more, anyway. 'There's been something I've been meaning to tell you and I don't think you're going to like it.'

Ivy stopped chipping at her black nail polish. 'What's that?'

'So, I was checking out Charlotte's yearbook footage and, well, you sort of make a cameo.' Olivia crossed her legs on top of Ivy's coffin.

'A goth in the yearbook film? Wow.' Ivy

frowned, seemingly impressed.

'It's not really like that. See, she sort of caught you in the background in Mister Smoothie when you broke that glass. It's a little vampalicious, if you know what I mean.'

'What?' Ivy jumped up. 'She saw me?'

'No, no. She didn't see you. I'm positive. But it *is* on camera.'

Ivy tugged at her hair, starting to pace. 'We have to get rid of it. We absolutely have to.'

'I know.' Olivia rested her chin on her fist. 'But how?'

Ivy walked the length of the room, hands in pockets. 'Good question. I mean, we can't just take it. Charlotte's actually been nice lately.'

'Right.' It was a mystery why, but the Queen of Mean had been unexpectedly pleasant over the past few days. 'We can't give her any reason to turn nasty again. I need all the allies I can get at school.'

'Exactly, which means this will have to be a covert op!' Ivy got on her knees and started digging through the DVDs inside the television stand.

'Does that mean I have to wear black?' Olivia examined her matching pink flannel pyjamas. Black was *so* not her colour.

'No,' said Ivy, still digging. 'We need to act natural.' She waved a couple of movies above her head. 'Found them!'

'Found what?'

'Our bedtime inspiration.' Ivy handed her sister the DVDs.

Spy movies! Three separate instalments of *James Bond.* 'I'll just call you Double-O-Ivy!' Olivia smiled.

'But first we need a strategy.'

Olivia grabbed a notepad and her fuzzy-topped pen, ready to jot down the plan.

'OK,' Ivy started. 'At the next committee

meeting, you need to distract Charlotte.'

Distract Charlotte, wrote Olivia. 'Got it!'

'Right, then I'll get the camera,' continued Ivy, 'so that I can delete the footage.'

Olivia jotted it down. 'Um, Ivy?' She gave her sister a mischievous grin. 'You know that means you'll have to attend a committee meeting, then?'

Ivy scrunched up her face. 'A necessary evil.'

Olivia giggled, reviewing the plan she had written in her notebook. 'It's sort of exciting, don't you think? I feel like we're in a heist movie!'

Ivy didn't laugh. She climbed into her coffin and crossed her arms across her chest. 'Let's just make sure we get the footage back.' Her sister's expression was dark. Olivia couldn't be sure whether it was Ivy's mood or a shadow cast by her coffin, but she was certain something was going on with her vampire twin.

What can it be?

Chapter Six

Ivy's mouth watered at the tantalizing smell of juicy T-bone steak cooking on Aunt Rebecca's outdoor grill. Thank goodness her dad had brought plenty of meat this trip. Aunt Rebecca was a vegetarian like Olivia and the Abbotts, and Ivy had just about died when she had last stayed at the ranch, with nothing but bunny food around. If she'd had to eat one more Vita Vamp bar in Aunt Rebecca's bathroom, she was sure she'd have been sick.

Outside, the sun was trickling through green leaves, spattering bright polka dots of light across her family's faces. Acorns littered the ground and the distant mooing of cows could be heard in the background. Even Ivy could appreciate the peacefulness of Aunt Rebecca's farm. She enjoyed the sweet scent of the hay scattered under their feet. She was just thinking how lucky she was to have everyone gathered in one place when she felt her stomach turn. She sniffed the air. *Is that garlic?*

Aunt Rebecca appeared out of the kitchen, carrying a tray. 'Four loaves of my famous garlic bread coming right up!'

Ivy could feel her face going pink. She wanted to faint at the idea of garlic-smeared bread. That was ten times worse than any bunny food. But what could she do? She couldn't tell Aunt Rebecca that almost every single person at the ranch was allergic to garlic. What were the odds of that?

Mrs Abbott licked her lips, taking a big whiff of the freshly baked bread. 'My favourite!'

Olivia's eyes bugged and she squeezed Ivy's hand underneath the table. 'Our grandparents!' said Olivia through gritted teeth. 'If they get anywhere near the garlic they'll pass out. There's not a speck of garlic to be found in all of Transylvania – they're not used to this. We have to keep the evil globes away from them!'

The Lazars' smiles were starting to look a little stretched and Brendan's sister Bethany was turning the colour of cooked shrimp. They needed a plan – and fast!

Ivy headed straight for the kitchen, signalling for Olivia and Brendan to follow. The fierce scent of garlic nearly bowled her over. She blinked hard, trying to focus.

Brendan looked close to losing his appetizers. 'Vampire kryptonite!' he said, wiping a layer of sweat off his forehead. 'Are they trying to kill us?' Ivy knew her boyfriend was exaggerating. A small taste of garlic would hardly be enough to poison them, but it was enough to make them feel deathly ill.

'I know,' said Ivy, pulling her sister and Brendan into a huddle. 'Consider this Garlic-CON 5! This is not a drill, people! Brendan, you find a baguette.' She pointed to the pantry. 'And I'll grab the butter. We'll make some fake garlic bread and pass that round the vampires.'

'Olivia can pass out the real garlic bread to anyone who can eat it,' suggested Brendan, sucking in his breath.

Olivia hesitated. 'Do you really think that will work?'

Ivy looked deadly serious. 'Brendan can use diversion tactics to provide cover if either of us needs it.'

'Diversion tactics?' Now Brendan was the one who was less than gung-ho.

Ivy sighed. 'OK, so I know the plan may be a bit sketchy, but it's the best I could come up with on such short notice. I'm not a mastermind.'

Olivia grinned. 'Are you sure about that?'

At that moment they heard the girls' grandmother calling for them. It sounded urgent.

'Right,' said Ivy, placing her hand in the centre of their human triangle. 'Are we in or are we out?'

'I'm in.' Olivia put her hand over her sister's.

'I'm in.' Brendan placed his large hand on top.

'Great, Operation Garlic Bread is a go! Now, break!' They tossed their hands in the air. Ivy and Brendan hurried to retrieve the supplies. Brendan sliced the flaky baguette while Ivy buttered. Olivia arranged the fake garlic bread neatly on a tray and, in hardly any time at all, they had created a non-toxic dish that looked exactly the same as Aunt Rebecca's famous-but-lethal garlic bread. The trio hustled outside, ready to serve.

'Aunt Rebecca, you've worked so hard,' Olivia exclaimed, a little too loudly, to give Ivy and Brendan their cue. 'Please, let us!' Olivia scooped up the tray of real garlic bread and began circling the table. As usual, Horatio couldn't resist getting in on the table-waiting, too. He passed out napkins and wiped up stray crumbs.

Her aunt enthusiastically took two pieces for her plate. 'Charles, please help yourself!'

Charles pulled at his collar. Brendan went into a fit of coughing. *Oh no, quick!* Ivy darted forwards with her platter of harmless bread, while Olivia moved down the table to her parents, the Abbotts.

'Olivia, will you go ahead and serve the Count and Countess first?' Aunt Rebecca called. Ivy froze. Her sister didn't seem to know what to do.

Brendan jumped to the rescue. 'Pardon me, Rebecca, I was wondering...' He scratched his head. 'Do you know how to do any country dances? See, I've always wanted to try. Could you show me?'

Aunt Rebecca looked Brendan up and down,

as he stood in his black, rail-straight jeans and burgundy button-down shirt. 'Really?' she asked.

Ivy fought back the laughter bubbling up in her throat. *That* was the first idea that came to Brendan? Country dancing?

Brendan's eyes flitted to Ivy as she served the plain bread to her grandparents. Mission accomplished. 'Oh, never mind.' He tried to back away, but Aunt Rebecca caught his wrist.

'Don't be silly!' she said, slapping her knee. 'I think it's a great idea.' Once upon a time, Aunt Rebecca had thought Brendan was a no-good teenage yob. Now, she'd clearly changed her mind.

Brendan fidgeted. 'We don't even have music, so it's OK. I'll just sit down.'

Ivy gave Brendan a wicked grin. 'I think I saw a guitar in the house.'

'I'll get it,' offered Ivy's father.

Brendan shot Ivy a 'Help me' look, but all she

could do was snigger. She loved Brendan, but this was going to be fun!

Mr Vega returned with the guitar. 'It's been a while, but I think I remember how to play.' He strummed a chord and, to Ivy's surprise, it actually sounded good. Olivia clapped as Mr Vega began to pick out a lively country tune, filling the air with music and laughter.

Aunt Rebecca and Brendan stood facing each other. 'Take my waist,' she said. 'And now my hand.' The two stood as if ready to waltz. Brendan looked like he would rather have eaten an entire clove of garlic. 'Two steps back. One step to the side. Two steps back and do-si-do.' Aunt Rebecca locked elbows with Brendan and together they skipped in a circle.

Ivy gave Olivia a thumbs-up. One mission down: one mission to go. Ivy just wasn't sure her boyfriend would ever forgive her.

Olivia skipped one of her checkers over Brendan's, taking it off the board. Olivia had already captured half of Brendan's pieces. She and Brendan were playing a game at the living-room table in Aunt Rebecca's house while Ivy had a quick riding lesson outside. Olivia spotted Ivy riding by, holding on to the saddle with a death grip. At least she was trying!

'Hey . . .' Olivia watched Brendan make his move on the board. 'Do you know what's been up with Ivy lately?' Olivia felt weird going to Ivy's boyfriend for information, but she had to get to the bottom of this! 'She's seemed distracted and yesterday she was on the VVV and wouldn't let me see what she was doing. That's a serious violation of Twin Code 101!'

Brendan squirmed in his seat. 'I have no idea what you're talking about.' His voice cracked and he cleared his throat. 'I mean, she seems fine to me at least.' Olivia wasn't so sure, but before she

123

could say as much, Brendan switched subjects. 'While we're talking about Ivy, though, I was wondering if you could maybe tell me what her favourite flower is. If you know it.'

Olivia twisted her mouth to the side, thinking. *What would Ivy's favourite flower be?* 'Honestly, I haven't got a clue. I don't really know if flowers are Ivy's thing. Why?'

'It's nothing. I, well, I just had a bit of a surprise planned for the school dance.' He looked sheepishly at her. 'Don't tell Ivy, will you?'

'The school dance!' She'd been so busy enjoying herself at the ranch, she'd forgotten to worry about how Jenny and the committee were getting on without her. Olivia pulled her phone out and switched it back on. 'Twenty missed calls!' She scrolled through the call log. 'And every one of them is from Jenny. Hold on, Brendan.' She held one finger up. 'I *have* to see what's going on.' Olivia was imagining booked-up caterers, horrible weather forecasts, and a sudden shortage of DJs in town when Jenny answered the phone on the third ring.

'Oh my goodness, Olivia, where have you been?' Jenny's words came out in one gush. 'They are *on* the board.'

'Who is on the board?' Olivia was struggling to catch up.

'Lucrezia, Melinda and Veronica, of course! They didn't even have to gatecrash the meeting – they're officially part of the committee now!'

Olivia almost dropped her phone. 'What!' Brendan watched her face, frowning.

'Apparently, Lucrezia spoke to her dad, who is on the board of governors, and Principal Whitehead has been forced to find a spot for the girls on the committee. It's a total nightmare. They're making all the decisions. All-pink food to go with an all-pink party – prawn toast, pink mousse, pink lemonade.'

Olivia bit the inside of her cheek. *That's not such a bad idea.*

'And worst of all: No Goths Allowed!'

Olivia gasped. Now that *was* a bad idea. How had this happened? The dance was turning into a total mess. Olivia put her head in her hands. She had no idea what to do and, worst of all, she couldn't even ask for twin help, since something seemed to be up with Ivy. But how could she possibly fix this on her own? One thing was for sure: she should not have come away. Olivia slid to the living-room floor, leaning her back up against the hard drywall.

'Knock, knock.' Aunt Rebecca poked her head in through the screen door. Rebecca had her hair in two braids and her riding boots pulled over a pair of tight black leggings. 'Olivia! What's wrong?'

Olivia wasn't sure she could utter a word without crying.

126

Brendan put an arm around her shoulders. 'Whatever it is, you can tell your aunt,' he said softly. For a moment, she wished Jackson could be with her.

Aunt Rebecca came to stand in front of them and held out a hand. 'Come on, Olivia. Let's go for a walk.' Gratefully, Olivia allowed her aunt to lead her out on to the porch and into the fields that surrounded the farmhouse. Birds sang in the trees and the sound of soft neighing floated on the air from the stables.

Right at this moment, Olivia never wanted to leave the ranch.

She never wanted to see those three horrible girls again.

Chapter Seven

Ivy swiped her thick canvas gloves against the trouser-leg of her jeans, smearing brown mud across the tough denim. Her riding lesson was over and she'd been cleaning the stables. Ivy kicked the rubber soles of her boots against a mouldy doorframe, shaking out a shower of caked dirt.

While Ivy wouldn't be making best friends with a horse any time soon, she was definitely improving. Today, Rebecca had even allowed her to trot. Ivy hung the horse's bridle on a peg. Aunt Rebecca had gone for a walk with Olivia and Ivy had volunteered to spend extra time outside helping with chores. She hadn't even broken out in hives at the thought.

But just as she was starting to get all Zen with her outdoor surroundings, Ivy's ears pricked. The pattern of the footsteps was familiar and, without turning, she motioned for her dad to join her.

'You thought you could trick me?' Ivy jammed her hands on her hips, pretending to be serious.

Mr Vega chuckled. 'Your hearing is getting better. That was the stealthiest walk I can do.'

Ivy knew this was a compliment, but it was hard to be too thrilled when the more super her powers got, the more likely it was that she'd have to attend finishing school. 'Can I just be a normal vampire?' she asked.

'Ah, come on.' Ivy's dad gently rumpled the top of her hair. 'I know you don't want to leave home or go to Wallachia Academy, but the skills you learn there can actually be quite useful. I learned a lot when I went there, you know. You might even enjoy it.'

Ivy took a step back. 'You think Wallachia is a good idea?' She hadn't thought her father had been as sold on her attending as the Count and Countess were. 'I thought you didn't care about tradition.' After all, Charles had married Ivy's human mother and that was the biggest break with tradition ever.

Mr Vega grabbed an armful of hay and started helping scatter it in the freshly cleaned stall. 'Not all traditions are bad, Ivy.' *I'm not saying they are*, she thought. For instance, she happened to like getting presents on her birthday very much – that was a great tradition. 'What you need to understand is that your powers are stronger than the average Franklin Grove vampire's and you may need some help finessing them.' Charles brushed the leftover hay off his trousers. He gave Ivy a careful look. 'It's only because we care –

because we want what's best for you. Otherwise, we'd never suggest leaving Franklin Grove.'

Ivy's mind flitted to the scene caught on Charlotte's video where she'd smashed a glass with her bare hands. Maybe she did need some help. 'Perhaps . . .' she said, her voice trailing off. But before she could complete her thought, Ivy doubled over, pushing her fingers into her ears. 'Ahhh!' she screamed as a head-splitting noise assaulted her ears. The horses neighed and stamped in response. The sound was so loud she started feeling light-headed and wondered if she was about to faint. Her knees hit the mulch.

Somewhere in the distance, she could hear footsteps. 'Is everything OK?' It was Brendan. He cupped her elbow, holding Ivy upright.

She looked around. 'What's going on?' Charles and Brendan weren't bent over like this, clutching their ears. Ivy's dizziness faded as the noise subsided and she was able to stand without feeling like she would black out. 'What was that sound?' she asked. *So much for the peacefulness of Aunt Rebecca's farm!*

Charles and Brendan glanced at each other and Brendan answered, 'Um, I think Mrs Abbott was just squealing at the cuteness of the ducks.'

Ivy's eyes got wide. *The ducks?* Ivy's super-vamp hearing really *was* working on overdrive. She gulped. *Looks like I really do need to learn to control my powers.*

🦇　　　🦇　　　🦇

Olivia walked the fence-line with Aunt Rebecca. The wet grass soaked through her sneakers, but the fresh air already seemed to be serving its purpose. Olivia's nerves were slowly unwinding and she was able to take deep breaths and enjoy the sweet smell of the honeysuckle. Aunt Rebecca strolled beside her, asking a question every minute or two.

Olivia pressed her palm to her heart. 'I swear.

This dance is going to make me lose my hair. It's turned into a total stress factory.'

Aunt Rebecca leaned in close, pinching a few strands of Olivia's dark hair. 'No,' she said, examining them. 'But you are turning a bit grey.'

'No!' Olivia snatched her hair and held it out in front of her face. 'Where?'

Rebecca squeezed Olivia's shoulder. 'Relax! I'm kidding.'

Olivia tried to give her aunt a reproachful look. 'Hair is not something to joke about.'

'Sorry.' Rebecca pretended to zip her lips. 'Now, explain to me what's going wrong.'

Olivia sighed. So much had happened since she'd first accepted the position as chairperson. 'There are these three girls – Lucrezia, Melinda and Veronica,' Olivia began. 'They are just plain mean, like evil-stepsister mean. They have forced their way on to the committee and now they're trying to make the whole dance pink. Worse, they want to exclude most of the school, and anyone that dresses like Ivy will be strictly blacklisted. How O-negative is that?'

She stopped. Olivia had been ranting so fast, she hadn't realised she'd borrowed a vampy phrase from Ivy.

'It's bad,' Olivia picked up, hoping Aunt Rebecca put her strange choice of words down to teen speak. 'I want everyone to be at the dance, wearing whatever colour they like. But how do I get around the Terrible Trio?'

Aunt Rebecca hummed thoughtfully. 'That's a tough one.' She walked with her hands in her pockets. 'Do you want to know what I think?'

'Absolutely.' Olivia wished that planning a school dance came with an instruction manual, but getting some grown-up advice seemed like the next best thing.

'Olivia, you are stronger than you give yourself credit for. I think you need to stand up to these girls and fight for what you think is right. It wasn't easy for me, buying back this farm, for instance. But I did it.'

Olivia imagined her aunt without a family, without any support, but still trying to play hardball against the bank that had taken back the property. 'Why did you do it?' she asked.

Aunt Rebecca's hair blew softly in the breeze. 'Because I knew I had to have this piece of family history back in our lives. Your mother and I grew up together here on this land. I knew it was the best thing to do and it turns out I was right. It's given us a place where our whole family can gather. And look at how Ivy has tried to be better around the animals. She's riding horses! She's learning! Everyone can do the best that they can, if they put their minds to it. If you think the pink plan is a bad idea, you should come up with a better one. You're the chairperson. Be pleasant, but stand your ground.'

Olivia ogled her aunt like she was a five-star general who'd just urged her into battle. Olivia had always thought Ivy got her tough streak from being a vampire, but now she was thinking that perhaps the toughness came from the human side of the family. And if that was the case, surely Olivia could be tough, too.

'I know you're right.' Olivia reached down and plucked a dandelion from the ground. Pondering, she twirled it between her fingers. 'But the atmosphere has become so bad. I don't know how I can fix it.' Olivia blew on the dandelion and the fluffy white of the flower scattered in the wind. She made a wish. *I wish for the perfect night.* And then she quickly added, *Complete with the perfect boyfriend.*

'You'll think of something,' Rebecca assured her. 'I remember when I was your age, your mother and I used to love holding big barn dances at the farm. Dancing with Brendan brought back a lot of memories. Dressing up in boots and hats and country cowgirl gear! Oh, those days were so fun.'

Olivia drew in a sharp breath. 'That's it! Aunt Rebecca, we can have a barn-dance theme! No one in Franklin Grove will expect it. Maybe that will bring everyone together!' Olivia gave her aunt a giant bear hug. Maybe it was a good idea to come away for the day after all.

New dance theme? Check! Now all she had to do was deal with the mean girls . . . and find out what was bothering Ivy . . . and talk to Jackson. *Gulp!*

🦇   🦇   🦇

Ivy scraped sawdust off the back of her trousers. *How utterly embarrassing.* Brendan wrapped his arm around her waist, holding her close. Ivy was so not into the damsel-in-distress thing, but she guessed if she had to be saved, it might as well be a goth-gorgeous guy with skin the colour of pure white marble and high cheekbones that made picture-perfect valleys in his handsome face.

Ivy glanced up at her boyfriend. 'I'm fine.' She pulled away. 'Really,' she said after seeing the worried look on Brendan's face. 'It's my super-strong powers acting up again.' *At all the wrong moments*, Ivy added in her head.

'Super-strong powers?' Brendan's eyebrows swooped up.

This was going to take some explaining. She looked to her father for help.

Charles gave a slight nod. 'You'll have to excuse me,' he said, clearing his throat, 'but I should go back to check on my parents.'

Ivy took Brendan's hand and led him to the big porch that wrapped around the main house, where they plopped down on one of the swing seats. Ivy let her boots dangle as Brendan pushed the swing back and forth, his fingers still curled around hers.

'When I told you about Wallachia Academy, I might have left out a few parts.'

'Oh?' Brendan's eyebrows shot up beneath his hair.

'Apparently my powers accelerate as I get older,' she told Brendan. 'It's a part of being one of the gentry of Transylvania. It's pretty freaky, really,' Ivy admitted. 'It doesn't happen to most vampires. I accidentally broke a glass in my bare hand at Mister Smoothie the other day.' Ivy laughed uncomfortably. 'So anyway, that's why I've been invited to finishing school – to learn to control them.'

'Ivy!' He stopped the swing. 'Then that absolutely means you have to go. If you know this about yourself, isn't it your duty to learn to control your powers? Do you want to risk blowing the vampire secret wide open?'

'Are you being serious? I thought you didn't want me to go.'

Brendan's smile faltered. 'I didn't want you to go, but that was before you told me about your powers.' He shook his head, staring out at the horizon.

'What's wrong? Why are you reacting like this?' Ivy asked.

Brendan's face was turning red. 'Can't you see, Ivy?' He said quietly. 'You owe it to everyone to learn to control your powers. If the vampire secret at Franklin Grove got out because you gave the game away, everyone would suffer.'

Ivy couldn't believe Brendan was making out she was in danger of letting down every vampire she knew.

'I'm sorry you feel that way,' she said.

Brendan turned to face her. 'It's not about how I feel. It's about the truth. I don't want you to be far away from me, but if it's for a really important reason . . .'

'We've never, ever argued before,' Ivy said,

sadness leaking through her.

'We're not arguing now.' Brendan's rigid expression softened. 'But I'm going to tell you when I think you're wrong.'

'So if we've never argued . . .' Ivy poked her finger into Brendan's ribs, trying to get him to laugh. She needed this mood to change super-fast. 'Does this mean I'm never wrong?'

Brendan swatted her away. 'This isn't funny, Ivy. For one thing, Olivia knows something's up and she's been asking me awkward questions. I don't want to be stuck in the middle. I mean, how bad does it have to be when one twin is asking the other twin's *boyfriend* what's going on? Please . . .' He pressed his palms together. 'For my sake as well as Olivia's, can you just come clean with your sister? If you do decide to leave the country, at least warn her. It might break a vampire rule, but I'm pretty sure you'll be breaking a much bigger twin-sister code if you sit back and do nothing.

You shouldn't be lying to your sister, no matter what your grandparents say.'

Ivy couldn't have been more surprised if Brendan had popped out of her coffin. He had never lectured her and she wasn't sure she liked him mixing the role of schoolteacher and boyfriend. Brendan pulled Ivy into his chest, but it felt clumsy instead of comfortable.

She felt his warm breath tickle her ear. 'It'll be fine,' he whispered. 'The two of us can enjoy one last perfect night at the dance before you leave for Transylvania. Deal?'

'Oh my darkness.' Ivy sat up straight. 'Now I know you're joking!'

Brendan looked like he'd been staked. His face got splotchy.

'What?' Ivy asked, confused.

Without a word, Brendan pushed off from the swing, shoved his hands in the pouch of his black sweatshirt and walked inside the house.

'Brendan!' she called. *Have I hurt his feelings about the dance? This is crazy!*

The screen door clattered shut behind him and any ounce of happiness leaked out of Ivy. Her boyfriend wasn't coming back. He thought she was wrong and that she was being selfish and that she should spend who-knew-how-long across the ocean at Wallachia Academy. She pushed the swing with the tips of her toes, staring at the empty spot beside her. Pinks, purples and oranges spread over the sky. As Ivy watched the beautiful sunset lighting up the ranch, she wondered: *How and when did everything start to go so wrong?*

Chapter Eight

'Can everyone please take a seat!' Wrangling a roomful of chatty girls was no easy task for Olivia. She was standing at the front of the common room, waiting to start the committee meeting, but the room was buzzing with so much excitement she could hardly get a word in! 'We only have a few days left, people!' She clapped several times. Chairs screeched, heels clacked, and at last it was quiet enough for Olivia to speak.

Before she began, Olivia chanced one quick glance at Lucrezia, Melinda and Veronica, sitting in the front row wearing three matching sneers. *Wait till they hear what I have to suggest.*

From the back of the room, Charlotte shot Olivia the thumbs up and the recording light blinked green. Into what weird universe had Olivia fallen that meant she was actually happy that Charlotte Brown had decided to attend another committee meeting after all? At least the camera would keep the Terrible Trio in check.

Fortunately for Olivia, that wasn't her only backup. Ivy had come along. Operation Delete Footage was on and Ivy was helping Charlotte in the hopes that she might have an opportunity to delete the vampy-looking footage.

'First,' Olivia began, 'I wanted to thank the committee for taking care of things while I was away and for the lovely suggestion of a pink theme.' Olivia watched as Lucrezia gave a smug flip of her hair. But Olivia wasn't done. 'And it was a lovely *suggestion.*' This time she emphasised the last word.

Olivia retrieved a folded sheet of paper from

her straw tote. 'This,' she fluttered the page so that everyone could see, 'is a copy of the committee contract that the principal had me sign when I took on this role,' Olivia said, silently thanking Jackson's manager, Amy, for always encouraging her to read the fine print. 'Here, in clause 2 of option 3, point 4 on the appendix for page 10 –' Olivia cleared her throat and began to read – '"The committee organiser shall take ultimate responsibility for all details of the dance, further to final approval by the principal."' She made a crisp fold in the paper and put it away.

Veronica twisted a string of chewed gum around her index finger. 'Translation?'

'I've already run an idea by the principal and it's been approved. This year's theme will be a barn dance and there will be absolutely no pink – and no black – whatsoever. Got it?'

The room erupted into howls of disappointment.

'But I already bought a pink skirt!'

'Does this mean I can't wear my fuchsia sundress?'

'Pink compliments my skin tone!'

Olivia shifted her weight on her feet. She hadn't expected her other classmates to be upset. She looked out into the small crowd. Even Jenny was shaking her head. Olivia had come this far and she wasn't turning back. Everyone needed to feel included and that meant putting a stop to anything and everything that could make people uncomfortable. *Right?*

Doing her best Ivy impersonation, Olivia stared down Lucrezia, Melinda and Veronica. 'Listen, I've made the decision – barn dance it is.' Before they could say anything, Olivia jerked her head in the direction of Charlotte's camera, daring them to argue. Thankfully, none of them did. Olivia's heart pounded. She'd done it. She had stood up for what she believed in. If she hadn't been wearing a skirt, she'd have performed a perfect straddle jump! 'OK, then,' she said, 'I want you all to go home and research ideas for food, music and decorations to fit the barn-dance theme, so that we can finalise details tomorrow. So, unless anyone has questions, I guess that's it for the day.'

The committee got to their feet. 'Dictator,' Olivia heard one girl mumble over her shoulder.

'Yeah, who does she think she is?' asked another.

Olivia's chin drooped. She had thought she was doing the right thing. 'Too much?' she asked, going over to Charlotte.

Charlotte removed the camera from its perch on her shoulder. 'Nah. Those girls needed putting in their places.' She raised her eyebrows and scanned Olivia from head to toe, as if seeing her for the first time. 'Seems like those three could actually learn a thing or two from *you*.'

From me? Do I really want to be a role model for bullies like that?

Thankfully, Olivia didn't have too much time to answer that big question because Ivy wandered over, her combat boots sticking out amongst the committee girls' dainty shoes like two black seeds in a giant pink watermelon.

'So?' Olivia probed her sister. 'Did Mission Deletion work?'

'Yeah, I took care of it when you were talking to Charlotte.'

This time Olivia really did jump up and down. 'Congratulations! Your secret's safe!' This was the best news she'd heard all day.

Ivy shrugged. 'For now.' She started to walk away.

'What is wrong with people today?' Olivia muttered, before following her twin out of the school.

🦇 🦇 🦇

Ivy jolted to a stop in the open doorway of her house on Undertaker Hill. *No way*. It looked as if a closet had exploded. Suitcases lay open with clothes spewing out on to the floor. Ivy even spotted one of her grandmother's fancy dresses hanging from a lampshade. The house was in total chaos. Olivia and Ivy stood in the doorway, bewildered.

'Maybe our dad shouldn't be skimping on a maid,' Olivia muttered into Ivy's ear. *Maybe you're right*, thought Ivy.

'Bombs away!' The girls looked up to see the Count tossing a velvet jacket over the top railing, where it landed in a lumpy pile with a number of other garments.

'What is going on?' Ivy demanded.

Horatio scrambled to fold the Count's clothing, but he couldn't keep up with the speed at which Ivy's grandfather was tossing articles down.

The Countess rushed in and stuffed a bag of toiletries into Horatio's stiff arms. Horatio offered the girls an awkward smile. 'The Countess can never have too many outfits,' he said, and then got back to work trying to wrestle the Count's clothes into a piece of leather luggage.

'Well, hello!' the Count shouted from the second floor, leaning over the railing. 'Didn't see you all there!'

Ivy snapped her neck back. 'No offence, but have you gone mad?'

The Countess scurried in with another bundle. 'Not mad; glad!' cried Ivy's grandmother. 'We have to get back to Transylvania at once!'

With surprising speed, the Count tramped down the stairs and began helping Horatio stuff the suitcase. 'Yes, without a single moment of delay,' he declared.

Ivy and Olivia's heads pinged back and forth between their grandparents.

'There's been an announcement. Prince Alex and Tessa have revealed their engagement.' The Countess wiggled the fingers of her left hand.

'Oh my goodness,' Olivia gushed. 'They're getting married?'

'Yes! And the Queen has asked specifically for me to help with the planning!' She glanced around at the floor. 'Now, where is my other shoe?' The Countess was clutching one lace-up boot in her slender hands.

Olivia dropped to the ground, crawling under the coffee table to retrieve the boot's mate. 'Wow,' she said, helping the Countess pack her fancy footwear. 'And I thought organising a school dance was tough! I can't imagine planning a royal wedding!'

'I know, and they are having the wedding in only a few weeks! *Weeks!*'

Ivy jolted at this. 'Why so soon?'

The Countess thrust another pair of shoes

into Horatio's arms and slung a belt over his shoulder. 'Apparently the Queen wants to get Alex and Tessa married as soon as possible to prove she really does support the two of them. The Transylvanian nobility seem to have gotten it in their heads that this isn't a real relationship.' The Countess clucked her tongue. 'And the Queen is eager to put those rumours to rest. So, the second Alex told her about the engagement, the Queen called me.' Then as if in confidence, she said to the girls, 'The Queen knows we're a bit more open-minded, what with all that business with Charles . . .'

Ivy was so not the type to get excited about anyone putting on a big, white meringue dress – that was more her sister's department – but even she had to admit she felt a rush of happiness for Tessa, the servant girl who'd been so kind to them in Transylvania. Tessa and the prince had been secretly in love for years and now she was being accepted into the Transylvanian royal family. Ivy. She could almost hear Olivia constructing her version of the fairy-tale romance now.

Ivy watched as Olivia sat on a suitcase to help Horatio lock it. Maybe there were good points to living in Transylvania. Despite the strict hierarchies, the Queen was going to a lot of trouble to prove that she accepted and supported her son's love. *Would finishing school really be all that bad?*

When the Count stepped back into the room, he appeared to have caught his breath. The suitcases were packed and the room was starting to look much more orderly. 'My dearest, we need to hurry if we're to catch our last-minute flight.' He turned to the twins. 'Are you two excited?'

'About what?' Ivy asked. 'I mean, I'm happy for Tessa and all. You'll have to promise to take pictures!'

'Naturally the two of you have also been

invited to the wedding,' said their grandfather.

'We have?' Olivia went gooey-eyed.

The Count pulled out two cream-coloured invitations, printed on thick stationery. Written in scrolling black calligraphy, the invitation read:

Together with their families
Prince Alexander of Transylvania
&

Miss Tessa Lupescu
Request the pleasure of your company as they
exchange wedding vows
In a summer ceremony
At the Chateau du Transylvania

'The Queen had these couriered over this morning,' explained the Count. 'We wanted you to get the full effect.'

Ivy watched her sister twirling around, and pressing her invitation tight to her chest. 'You're

thinking about dresses, aren't you?' she asked
Olivia.

'There are just so many possibilities!' Olivia
said, performing an impromptu waltz.

Ivy rolled her eyes and her grandfather leaned
in. 'You know,' he whispered. 'There will be
plenty of wedding cake for midnight feasts . . .'

'Red velvet cake?' Ivy gave the Count a sly
sidelong glance.

'I wouldn't doubt it.' They both licked their lips.

The Countess snapped shut the ruby-jewelled
clasp on her large shoulder bag. 'I'm ready!'
She held out her arms. 'Girls, we have your
flights booked and we will see you again soon.
It's going to be – what do you call it, Olivia? –
"fun and fabulous"!' The girls giggled at their
grandmother's hip lingo.

Horatio ushered the Count and Countess
out of the doorway, where a more human-sized
driver stood next to a shiny black Rolls Royce.

Why isn't Horatio taking them? Ivy wondered.

Hiking up her long skirt and bustling to the car, the Countess called back, 'Don't forget to help Ivy and Olivia with their packing, Horatio. Ivy will have more luggage than she can handle!'

Car doors slammed and the Rolls Royce rumbled to life, edging its way out of the circular drive and into Ivy's cul-de-sac. *Phew! Did any of that really happen?* It was such a whirlwind, Ivy wasn't sure.

Linking arms, Ivy and Olivia turned and followed Horatio back up the path and indoors.

'Excuse me,' said Olivia, nudging Ivy, 'but I thought *I* was the clothes horse. Why would *you* have more luggage than you could handle?'

Ivy bit her lip. She thought about inventing a story – *something about needing new clothes?* – but she stopped herself. She couldn't take this any longer. Brendan was right. She couldn't lie to her twin sister. 'How about we go up to our room? There's something I need to tell you.'

Horatio closed the front door behind them and Ivy followed her sister upstairs. Ivy knew the butler had to have overheard. Would Horatio be upset if she broke a vampire law? At the top of the staircase Ivy paused, peering over the railing. Instead of looking disappointed in her, Horatio just gave Ivy a solemn nod. *Right*, Ivy thought, *twin-sister code* does *trump vampire code. I can do this.*

'Now explain one more time.' Olivia sat cross-legged on Ivy's carpet.

'Olivia!' Ivy had already explained Wallachia Academy and why she needed to go three separate times. On the last one she had even gone so far as to include her grandparents' description of the Gothic castle!

'Sorry, I just can't believe it.' Olivia rested her elbows on her knees and tucked her fists under her chin. 'You're going to finishing school . . . in Transylvania . . . without me?' Olivia shook her head slowly. 'But, you know, that's not the worst thing. The worst thing is that you kept it a secret all this time. A secret! What other stuff has been going on behind my back?' Olivia's sharp green eyes bored into her sister.

Ivy groaned. She couldn't have felt worse if she were forced to eat bunny food for the rest of her life. 'That's it – I'm not going!' She tossed up her hands. Hadn't her grandparents ever heard of home-schooling? That was what she needed – Wallachia Academy-style.

Olivia's face was buried in her hands and her shoulders began to shake. Was she crying? Ivy's chest throbbed. She pulled Olivia's hands away from her face, expecting to see black streaks of mascara and splotchy make-up running down her cheeks, but – *wait!* – Olivia was . . . laughing!

'Gotcha.' Olivia grinned.

'Hey!' Ivy pushed Olivia's shoulder and she toppled over backwards so that Olivia was giggling on her back, legs up like an upside-down cockroach on the floor.

'What?' said Olivia, this time wiping real tears from her eyes. 'I knew something was up by the way you've been distracted, but I had no idea it was an opportunity this amazing.'

'Are you sure?' Ivy smiled uncertainly.

'Of course!' Olivia sat up. 'What's a few weeks over the summer anyway? You'll be back in Franklin Grove before either of us knows it.'

Ivy's smile fell. 'The summer? But Olivia, it might be longer than that if the teacher's assessment –' *Too late*.

Olivia was already out of the room and bounding down the stairs two at a time. 'Dad! Dad!' She called to their father, who was just setting his briefcase down in the entryway. 'I heard the good news! Ivy's going to super-vamp school.

How cool is that? My sister is a super-vampire!'

Upstairs, Ivy felt anything but super. She sank on to Olivia's bed. *Oh no, Olivia doesn't totally get it.* Ivy could be gone way longer than one summer . . .

Chapter Nine

*H*ere we go, Olivia thought as she studied her notes for the final committee meeting:

Bales of hay
Streamers
Country music
Anyone know a good line dance?

She had worn her favourite pink dress, freshly ironed and fitting just right. Olivia usually felt her best in pink and, today, she needed all the confidence she could muster. The committee had been strangely quiet since her announcement of the barn-dance theme. She hadn't received one call from Jenny and her email inbox was completely empty. Now Olivia was stuck sitting alone in the all-purpose room, waiting for her own meeting to begin. It really was lonely at the top!

Her cell phone vibrated. It was Jackson! Olivia did the maths in her head. If today was Thursday, then that meant Jackson must be in . . . Utah. She had memorised his itinerary, complete with interesting factoids she could share about each of his destinations. *Utah, 'The Beehive State'. Home to five national parks!*

Olivia answered the phone in a rush of excitement. 'Jackson! Oh my goodness, I'm beyond thrilled to hear from you.' She hadn't realised how much she needed to talk to somebody. 'I have so much to tell you.' The words spilled out of her. 'Wait, where are you?' There seemed to be a lot of shuffling in the background.

'Um . . .' Static came over the line. 'I'm in a

restaurant. It's a competition to help promote the film – a prize draw to go for dinner with the star.'

'You're eating with a total stranger?' Olivia shrugged. She didn't care who got to share nibbles with him, as long as she got to talk to him. 'Everything with the committee has been going absolutely haywire.'

'Huh?' Jackson's voice was distant over the phone, like he might have Olivia on speaker. Ew, she hated being on speakerphone.

'Haywire. It's been going haywire,' she shouted, glad the common room was still empty. 'The committee.'

'Oh right. What committee was that again?'

Olivia palmed her forehead. 'Jackson! You know which committee. The dance!' This conversation was clearly headed for a dead end. She tried switching tacks. 'Bad news, though: Ivy is leaving for the entire summer.'

There was a lull on the other end and then

Jackson asked, 'Cool, where are you two going?'

'We? No, Ivy is going, not me. I'm going to have twin-teration anxiety.' Olivia cringed at her bad joke. She waited again. 'Jackson?'

Then Olivia heard something to put a stake through any girl's heart. "Zis will match ze colour palette much better.' A girl's voice, and in a French accent, no less!

Parlez-vous 'buzz kill'? thought Olivia drily.

'Hey, Olivia . . .' Jackson was back on the line. 'I have to run, sorry. My wardrobe manager wants to show me some pictures of outfits for my appearance.'

The line went dead and Olivia was left staring at a blank screen. What was going on with Jackson? He had always said he didn't care about wardrobe as long as he didn't look ridiculous. The boy actually hated shopping. Sometimes Olivia wondered how they could be such a good match! So why was he discussing outfits when he was meant to be out for dinner with a fan?

The committee started to file in, something that should have made Olivia feel less lonesome. One of the members hollered an enthusiastic 'Yeehaw!' in honour of the barn-dance theme.

Olivia gave a half-hearted 'Yeehaw' in return. But it was tough to be a cheerful cowgirl when she had the boyfriend blues.

Rather than their usual seats front-and-centre, Lucrezia, Melinda and Veronica took the back row, leaning backwards in their chairs and popping big gobs of green gum. *Could they look any less interested?* Olivia wondered. She ignored them, put her phone away, and started the meeting.

'Congratulations, you guys!' Olivia tried to force her peppiest smile. 'This is our very last committee meeting!' She had expected cheers, but all she got was radio silence.

One of Lucrezia's bubbles made a loud crack and the two other girls giggled.

Olivia felt her fingernails dig into her skin. 'Cut it out, you three,' she snapped.

Lucrezia stood up, wiping the bubble gum from the corners of her mouth. 'Who do you think you're talking to?' Lucrezia jutted her hip as if daring Olivia to answer. She didn't. 'We're a grade older and it's about time you learned your place, even if you are the chairperson.' The three girls started to strut to the front of the room. Was Olivia about to become the Terrible Trio's next victim . . . in front of everyone? 'We'll be taking over from here on in, thank you very much.'

In the background, Olivia noticed a figure appear in the doorway – Jenny! 'Excuse me a minute,' Jenny said, pleasantly but firmly.

That was so not the Jenny Olivia remembered. Everyone in the room quietened down. Olivia had never seen Jenny so – *what was the word?* – confident before. Smile in place, Jenny strode up the aisle straight to the front of the room, Charlotte in tow.

Charlotte sidled up to Olivia. 'I've been giving Jenny a few pep talks. Watch and be amazed.'

'Pep talks?' Olivia was still trying to process this sudden turn of events.

'Check it out.' Charlotte opened her tote bag and let Olivia peek inside, where a well-thumbed hardback of *Stand Up for Yourself (And Don't Take any Garbage)* was hiding, speckled with a dozen colourful post-its. 'Taught me everything I know about life.' Charlotte slid the tote back over her shoulder.

That book explains Charlotte's attitude? Olivia didn't know what to say. Charlotte may have been a bit, *ahem*, overzealous with her confident attitude in the past, but as Olivia looked at Jenny squaring her shoulders at the Terrible Trio, she thought the strategy seemed to be working quite well for Jenny at least.

'Lucrezia, Melinda, Veronica.' Jenny's voice didn't wobble once. 'I have news for you. You may not be in charge of the dance. But . . .' she paused, 'you can be in charge of the dance refreshments. After all, your drink mixes were to die for last year. The committee would love you to whip up something similar for the dance this year. How does that sound?'

'You mean it?' Melinda asked.

Lucrezia's perfectly pink lips pulled into a genuine smile. 'We came up with that recipe all by ourselves last year.'

Olivia couldn't believe what she was witnessing. *Was that all it took?* All this time and the only thing those girls needed to feel valued was an area of responsibility? Olivia had made a rookie mistake, and she was usually so good with people! *Why didn't I think of that? Maybe this whole Jackson issue has been distracting me more than I thought.*

In a snap, Jenny had zapped the problem. She

came over to Olivia. 'I'm sorry for unloading so much responsibility on you. It wasn't fair, but now I'm here to help. OK?'

'Thank goodness.' Olivia blew out a sigh of relief.

'Great.' Olivia noticed that, for the first time, Jenny's mousy-brown hair was pulled back away from her face. 'And now that I actually have an opinion, the first thing I can help with is the theme.' *Not this again*, thought Olivia. 'Do you really want to impose a barn-dance theme on everyone?' Jenny asked. 'Wouldn't you rather make sure everyone dressed how they wanted? The whole point was to make sure everyone was happy and comfortable, wasn't it?'

'You're right!' Olivia's heart sank. 'Oh my goodness.' She really had been a dictator. And worse, she hadn't even been trying!

'May I have your attention?' Olivia rapped her knuckles on one of the tables, trying not to

170

cringe at the collective groan that rippled through the room. She noticed some of the committee members were already wearing cowboy hats. She didn't want to disappoint them twice. She took a deep breath. 'What about a barn dance, but with a pink-and-black theme?' she proposed. 'The girly girls can be pretty in pink and the goths can feel included, too. Plus, everyone can have fun with gingham!'

The committee broke into whoops and squealing; a big step up from the ghostly silence following Olivia's last announcement. As people started texting their friends in excitement, Olivia felt her cheeks blush with a new burst of energy. She was back on track.

'Much better!' she beamed. 'Next thing on the list: how would you guys like to come back to my house so that we can hammer out the finer details over pizza? Sound good?' The room erupted into cheers.

Olivia led the way out to the parking lot, walking ahead of a pair of girls planning their outfits. 'OK, which earrings will go best with my pink hat – the pale crystal hoops or the chandelier earrings?'

With a quick stab, Olivia remembered the French accent in the background during Jackson's call advising him that *something* would match the colour palette better. What colour palette? And, more importantly, what could her boyfriend be up to?

When no one answered at the Abbotts', Ivy jiggled the doorknob and let herself inside. She wiped her boots on the cheery 'Welcome' mat before stepping on to the plush white carpet of the Abbotts' foyer. If Ivy's house had a polar opposite, it was Olivia's. Where the Vega house had curtains made of dark velour, the Abbotts' drapes boasted a bright floral pattern. And unlike the deep crimson of Ivy's walls, Olivia's were painted a pale sky blue. Ivy sometimes wondered how the Abbotts ever got any sleep at all, what with their whole decor theme reminding her of a dazzling summer morning.

'Olivia?' she said, rounding the corner. 'Oh. My. Darkness.' Bunny-mania had taken over the Abbott residence. There were pink-clad girls everywhere! A clump of girls was crowded on to the sofa, squashed one against the other, making paper chains and bunting out of scraps of gingham.

Ivy was even more shocked to see the Terrible Trio sitting at Olivia's kitchen table, sipping from etched glass cups and diligently taking notes. *Who tamed those beasts?* Ivy wondered.

She spotted Olivia sitting on the floor, surrounded by committee members, patiently making decorations out of hay and pink-and-black papier mâché. Olivia glanced up. 'Hi!' She beamed, standing up and picking her way through the various dance-related obstacles. 'Welcome to the mad house!'

'Olivia, I don't know how to tell you this, but . . .' Ivy eyed her sister seriously. 'There is hay in your home.'

'I know!' Olivia led her sister into the entryway, one of the only chatter-free zones in the house. 'Isn't it crazy? New plan: we're going to have a pink-and-black theme for the barn dance. Isn't it perfect? Even you will be happy. Pick any fabulous black outfit in your wardrobe and you can wear it, no problem.'

Ivy let her head droop to the side. 'Great,' she said drily. 'Thanks for that. I'm, like, so excited to indulge my inner goth.' Ivy displayed wiggling jazz-hands with zero enthusiasm.

Olivia's smile fell. Even her hair looked flatter. 'What's wrong?'

'Look, you know I love you and I'm glad you're having fun on the committee, but honestly, do Brendan and I look like the type of people who would enjoy a school dance?'

'Er, Ivy?' Olivia chewed her fingertip. 'I think you might have yourself a Brendan-sized problem.'

'What do you mean?'

'Well, don't you remember how Brendan looked like he'd sucked a lemon drop when you dissed the school dance?'

Ivy shifted in her boots. 'Um, yeah, I guess.' Then something else floated to the front of her memory. She flinched. 'There might have been another incident.' Ivy slapped her hands over her eyes, peeking through her fingers at Olivia. 'There was a phone conversation. Brendan tried to suggest I might enjoy the dance and then . . . oh and then . . . the look on his face at Rebecca's ranch!'

175

'What face?'

'A face like I had crushed his thumbs with a hammer. How could I have been so dense? He's really up for it, isn't he?' *Kill me now*, thought Ivy, only she wasn't sure if it was because she had hurt Brendan or because she might actually have to attend the dance.

'He cares about you. *Hello?* Why wouldn't he want to be seen with you on his arm at the school's most romantic event ever?'

That's it. Olivia's right. I have to make this up to Brendan. So what if dances weren't her thing? Her boyfriend was! She climbed over the girls on the floor making miniature cowboy hat name badges.

Olivia followed behind her, heaving a sigh of pleasure upon seeing the new decorations. 'I wish I could have a pink rhinestone cowboy hat for the dance. Wouldn't that be awesome?'

Ivy was only half-listening. 'Olivia, I need to

borrow your phone. I left mine in my backpack at home.' *With night as my witness, I, Ivy Vega, will make this better.*

'Sure, of course,' Olivia told her.

Ivy shooed girls away, lifting cushions and searching for Olivia's purse.

'But, here's the thing,' continued Olivia, now in full-on daydream mode. 'How am I going to organise getting a pink cowboy hat alongside everything else I have to do? It's impossible!'

'Olivia!' Ivy flung a cushion on to the floor. 'One problem at a time, please.'

'Right, sorry.' Olivia fished through a layer of hay. 'Found it!' She held her purse over her head, delivering it to Ivy.

Ivy's thumbs punched in her text to Brendan: *Will you do me the honour of being my partner at the dance? Love, Ivy.* The green bar slid across the bottom of the screen. She almost couldn't look. *Message sent!*

'Did I really just do that?' She stared open-mouthed at the screen.

Olivia wrapped her arms around Ivy's stomach and squeezed. 'Yes, because you really care about Brendan. Admit it.' She poked her sister. 'You might just have a bit of fun, too.'

The phone chirped. The message read: *Killer. For sure!*

'That's that.' Ivy handed the phone back and dusted her hands together. 'Guess I'm going. But promise me,' she said, as she scanned the room full of giggling girls, 'I won't become like that.'

Olivia laughed. 'There is no chance you will ever be like that, silly! Brendan loves you just the way you are.'

All of this fuss over her relationship with Brendan, and Ivy had completely forgotten that her sister was without her boyfriend. 'Have you heard from Jackson recently?'

Olivia frowned. 'Yes.'

'But . . .' Ivy prodded her twin.

'But he had a French wardrobe manager with him and had to hang up.'

By the deathly pale look on her sister's face, Ivy guessed that the wardrobe manager had sounded a bit too girly for Olivia's taste. 'I wish there was something I could do,' said Ivy, frustrated. 'Why don't vampy superpowers come with a boyfriend-summoner? Something that would actually be useful!'

Olivia smoothed her hair and clothes, straightening her posture. 'No biggie. I'll be fine. I'll have to be if I'm going to spend the whole summer without you, as well as without Jackson.'

The summer? Ivy stared at her toes, wanting to tell Olivia the truth. It could be more than a summer: a lot more. Ivy scuffed her boot on the floor. She might not be able to avoid going away herself, but maybe there was something else she could do . . .

Chapter Ten

Olivia blinked against the sunlight pouring in through the slats in her whitewashed shutters. She peeled her head off the pillow, bleary-eyed. Yesterday had been exhausting. Olivia wouldn't care if she never saw another pink-and-black paper chain in her life – or at least until tonight. Her vision came into focus and her breath caught.

At the foot of her bed was a pair of pink cowboy boots, the exact same as the pair she'd been dreaming about. *Wait – am I still asleep?* The boots had loopy white embroidery and perfectly pointed toes. She rubbed her eyes . . .

and the boots were still there! Pushing back the down comforter she reached for the soft pink leather. They were real! Tucking them under her arm, she ran downstairs to the kitchen, where her parents were sipping coffee and sharing a newspaper.

'Who put these in my bedroom?' Olivia held out the pink cowboy boots like she was presenting a prized possession for 'show and tell'.

Her mother batted her eyes, sharing an exaggerated shrug with her father. 'Why, I have no idea. It has nothing to do with us.'

It looked like her parents could use a few acting lessons. Olivia could see right through their innocent façade, but before she could question them any further she heard the sound of her perky ringtone coming from upstairs.

'Hold that thought,' she told her parents, racing back to her bedroom. She answered her phone, breathless. 'Hello?'

'How do you like the boots?' asked a deep, dreamy voice on the other end.

'Jackson!' *Of course!* 'How did you know to buy me pink boots? I was just dreaming about them and now, here they are . . . in my room!' Olivia was beginning to think that acting wasn't his only area of expertise. Perhaps her boyfriend was a mind reader, too.

'I had them couriered over. Thought you'd like something special for the dance.'

'But how . . . but how . . .' Olivia sucked in her breath. 'Did my sister call you?'

'Oh, Olivia.' She could picture Jackson's eyes twinkling with laughter. 'You sure are slow on the uptake sometimes.'

Olivia made a mental note to give her sister a bone-crushing hug for this. 'There's only one more thing that would make this dance complete.' Well, other than the rhinestone hat. Not that she would mention that to Jackson.

'And what would that be?' asked Jackson, still chuckling.

Olivia walked by the mirror, saw her hair sticking up at crazy angles, and immediately ducked. Thank goodness her hot boyfriend couldn't see her with bed-head!

She recovered, remembering with a sad sigh that Jackson was a safe distance away in Utah. 'If I had my boyfriend as my date,' she finished. There wasn't a peep on the line. Olivia could hear her own breath echoing through the receiver. 'Jackson? Hello, Jackson!'

'Olivia, the promo tour has been extended. I'm so sorry, but I've been invited to a live TV interview in Boston and I couldn't turn it down. I don't know what to say. You understand, right? That's why I bought the boots, to make it up to you.'

The boots were beautiful, but they didn't stop Olivia's heart from dropping down into her slippers. 'Is that why you had a wardrobe manager with you the other day when we talked?'

'Er . . . yes, yes – that's exactly it.' Olivia heard shuffling around on Jackson's end. 'Hey, Olivia?' He sounded distracted now. Olivia knew his distracted voice. 'I have to go. We'll talk later, OK? Bye!'

Olivia didn't even get to say 'goodbye' before the dialling tone was droning in her ear. 'Talk to you later,' she mumbled to no one, letting the phone slip on to her mattress. Fat, salty tears started to pool on her eyelids. Her boyfriend was doing everything right. He remembered to phone. He sent presents. *So why do I feel so wretched?* Olivia wondered.

The phone rang again and Olivia picked it up, hoping it was Jackson ringing her back. It wasn't.

'Don't sound so happy to hear from me,' said Ivy.

'Sorry,' said Olivia, flopping on to her cool sheets. 'I thought you were someone else.'

'Jackson?'

'Maybe.' Olivia stared up at the ceiling and wiped the last few tears from the corners of her eyes. 'What's up?'

'I was wondering if you wanted some help getting everything ready for the dance. I think it's going to be deadly. I mean it!'

Olivia felt another lump rise in her throat. 'That's, like, the kindest thing anyone's ever offered to do for me,' she blurted.

Ivy laughed. 'I think you're just feeling a little fragile today, but, either way, there isn't anywhere else I'd rather be. Not only will we get all the decorations for the dance up on time, but I will personally make sure that we both manage to look drop dead.'

Olivia hung up the phone, feeling a glow of warmth for her sister. After all this preparation, she couldn't believe it – it was nearly time for the dance!

🦇   🦇   🦇

As she and Olivia got closer to Franklin Grove, it was as if every fibre of Ivy's vampire-being was rebelling against the very idea of a school dance. Ivy stared out the window of her dad's shiny black sedan, feeling seriously grave about the prospect of doing any dancing at all.

She had spent the day – a *whole* day – helping Olivia get herself and the dance ready. Of course, Ivy wanted to do everything she could to cheer her sister up. After all, Olivia thought her boyfriend didn't care about her. But Ivy had to confess that spending the day with her hair in rollers while hanging bunting and tying balloons was going above and beyond the call of duty.

Olivia drummed her cerise-painted nails on the back seat. The tiny diamante stickers she'd applied on top of the polish shimmered in the dim light.

'It's going to be fine.' Ivy examined her own nails. She'd opted for a more classic goth black.

'I know, I know.' A worried crease formed at the top of Olivia's nose. 'I just want everyone to have a good time!'

'They will!' Ivy assured her. Olivia eyed her sister and Ivy knew Olivia was particularly sceptical about *her* attitude. 'Even me!' Ivy exclaimed. 'I mean, look at me.'

Ivy had zipped home to change before picking up Olivia, and was now dressed in skinny black jeans, a black-and-white gingham shirt with patch pockets, a black cowboy hat, and an authentic leather shoestring tie around her neck. Ivy had embraced the theme and put her own spin on it, just like Olivia had wanted.

'You're the best gothic cowgirl I've ever seen!' Olivia nodded approvingly.

'I'm the *only* gothic cowgirl you've ever seen.'

'Still! OK, how do I look?' Olivia pouted her lips and turned her head from side to side for Ivy to examine.

'Fluffy?' Ivy admired the pink cowgirl outfit. Olivia wore a puffy, layered ra-ra skirt that Ivy wouldn't be caught dead in, but it looked très cute on her sister. Olivia's shirt was knotted at the front and her hair was tied into pigtails with two puffy pink hairbands. 'And your boots, they totally make the outfit!'

'You think so?' Olivia beamed. 'After all that Hollywood glamour, it's sort of nice to dress up in an outfit that's actually fun.'

That much Ivy could agree with. Although she had adored her outfit for the awards ceremony — a gorgeous black kimono embroidered with delicate red dragons — she *had* felt a bit constricted. She would take jeans over a fitted gown any day.

Mr Vega edged the sedan's wheels up to the curb. 'You girls both look stunning. Ivy, coffin by ten, OK?'

But Ivy was distracted. She had spotted Brendan standing in front of the school's gates, right between the big iron initials 'F' and 'G'. He strode towards the car in his shiny black cowboy boots and slender grey slacks. Ivy had never seen her boyfriend look so tall, dark and drop-dead handsome. He opened the door and, like a true gentleman, helped both Ivy and Olivia out of the car.

'This is for you.' He presented a corsage to Ivy made of deep purple . . . thistle! Even she had to admit, it was perfect. He helped pin it to her gingham shirt and then held out the crook of his arm so that Ivy could slip her hand through.

The other arm he extended to Olivia, and together the three of them walked into the crowd of students dressed in pink-and-black cowboy outfits. Ivy squeezed Brendan's arm. *Olivia has totally pulled it off!* She peeked around Brendan. *Does Olivia look OK?* Ivy didn't want her sister to feel lost without Jackson, but from the moment Brendan opened the school's doors, Olivia was surrounded by a swarm of adoring classmates.

'This theme is the best!' said a red-handkerchiefed boy, patting Olivia on the back.

'Oh my goodness, have you seen the bales of hay in the hall?' Ivy recognised Jenny from the committee. 'You just have to! Come on!'

Ivy was amazed to discover that Olivia had her own mini paparazzi. *If only Jackson could see his girlfriend in action!* Olivia led the way into the assembly hall and both twins gasped. It looked even better than when they had left to get changed. The gingham bunting was now hanging from the rafters and dance-goers were filtering in beneath a pink-and-black balloon arch. Inside the hall, everyone was sitting on hay bales and a country-and-western band was playing. Olivia had covered every detail, from floor to ceiling.

'I can't believe you managed to tame the beasts.' Ivy pointed to Lucrezia, Melinda and Veronica. They were busy handing out berry-bright fruit punch, no attitude included.

'Actually, that was Jenny's idea.' Olivia had her hands on her hips as she surveyed the rest of the transformed dance hall.

Ivy shrugged. It was hard to be a gothic grump when everyone was having so much fun. Ivy had better be careful that she didn't let a 'Yeehaw!' slip out accidentally. Even better was the fact that Olivia seemed delighted, despite the fact that Jackson was a no-show. Ivy felt the familiar stab of guilt. *How delighted will Olivia be when she finds out I might be away for more than the summer?* Ivy tried to bury the thought.

'May I have the honour of this dance?' Brendan offered his hand with a flourish.

Ivy bit her lip, glancing in the direction of her sister, who was trying out the hay bales with a group of girls from the committee.

'Olivia's fine! Come on!' He took her hand and dragged Ivy out on to the dance floor. In perfect step with the music, Brendan twirled her and circled in an excellent version of a do-si-do.

'Where did you pick up these moves?' asked Ivy. Her dark hair was flying and she was spinning, spinning, spinning until she was dizzy. If Ivy wasn't mistaken, she was actually having – *gasp!* – fun. That was the last thing she'd expected.

Brendan pulled Ivy closer, looking a bit sheepish as he stared down at her. 'Er, I might have been practising the country dancing your Aunt Rebecca taught me.'

That had to be the sweetest thing Ivy had ever heard and it didn't even make her nauseous. She gazed up at Brendan, with his intense dark eyes and cute shaggy hair. Would he still love her when she was so far away? He smiled, warm and familiar. Ivy smiled back and, somehow, she had a feeling that everything would be fine.

Chapter Eleven

Olivia had once landed a perfect round-off back handspring with a full twist at her school's homecoming game, but pulling off this dance had been ten times harder . . . and better! She watched Ivy line dancing with Brendan and a mixed group of goths and bunnies. *I knew that she'd have fun if she gave the dance a chance!*

She only had one extra wish. Olivia squeezed her eyes shut, clicked the heels of her fabulous pink boots, and wished for Jackson to be with her. But when she opened her eyes again, she was still alone. *Hey, a girl has to try.*

A sudden scuffling sound caught Olivia's

attention and she whirled around to see three girls blocking the end of the balloon archway. She glanced at the punch bowl. It was abandoned. Oh no, she knew taming the Terrible Trio had been too easy!

Olivia rushed over to Lucrezia, Melinda and Veronica to see what was causing the fuss. 'Can I help you guys with something?'

Lucrezia stepped back and Olivia was stunned to see Camilla – just back from Paris and dressed as a space-cowboy character. *Probably from one of her favourite sci-fi books*, thought Olivia. Camilla had donned a fishbowl helmet over her Stetson, and even Olivia had to smile at her friend's eccentricity.

Melinda, on the other hand, looked disgusted. 'She cannot come in looking like that.' Melinda swished her hand over Camilla as if she were something Olivia should be able to clean up. 'She's not dressed for the theme.'

Olivia frowned. 'You guys, have you learned nothing?' She caught Jenny's eye from across the dance floor and Jenny headed straight over, arriving in front of the group looking as self-assured as a real, live sheriff.

Jenny pushed her white cowboy hat down over her head. 'Lucrezia, Melinda, Veronica, it is not your job to be refusing people entry. Your job is to attend to the refreshments.' She pointed at the unmanned beverage table. 'And you've abandoned it. Remember what we talked about?'

Olivia nodded at Jenny. She had provided first-rate backup, but this time Olivia could tell it wasn't going to be enough.

'Look,' Olivia stepped up. 'Tonight is all about letting people have fun. Relax a little. Maybe you can all join the line dance together,' she suggested, knowing this might be asking too much too soon.

Veronica shrieked. 'Relax! Weren't you the one

trying to dictate what theme we should have in the first place?'

'Hey!' Camilla stomped her space-inspired snow boots. 'I will not have you girls compromise my artistic integrity. I am a fangirl,' she shouted, through the thick plastic of her helmet, 'and I'll come wearing whatever I want!'

Lucrezia raised her eyebrows at Olivia, ignoring Camilla. 'Veronica's right. You're the one who insisted on this theme. What a hypocrite.'

Olivia wanted to tear out her hair. She knew they had a point, but she'd learned her lesson since then and she didn't want to be pulled off course again. She reached past the line of girls, lunging to try and help Camilla get in. 'Follow me,' she told Camilla.

But as she reached out, Lucrezia bumped shoulders with Olivia and the three of them got caught up, staggering in a big heap towards the balloon arch. Olivia felt the arch sway behind her and Camilla landed on top of Olivia with a sharp elbow to her stomach. 'Ouch!'

Pop! Pop! Pop!

Olivia flinched as balloons burst in loud, crackling rounds. The archway sagged crookedly, making Olivia wish she could sink straight into the floor. *We're ruining the dance!* Olivia sat up, straightening her knotted shirt, scared to see how many students were staring.

Jenny helped Olivia to her feet. 'Are you OK?'

'I am,' said Olivia, patting down her ruffled skirt. 'But I think my pride might have taken a few hits. Is everyone looking?'

Jenny pressed her lips together, looking shifty. 'No, no, not too bad.'

Olivia's heart plummeted. 'Thought so.' This made the second event today that Olivia was glad her boyfriend hadn't been there to witness. With every ounce of confidence she could muster, Olivia walked back up to the Terrible

Trio. 'Girls . . .' Olivia borrowed Ivy's best death squint. 'If you don't start behaving, I'm going to have to ask you to leave.'

Melinda studied her flawless French manicure. 'See, you guys?' It would have been impossible for Melinda to look haughtier if she was part of the royal family. 'There's that rule book again — coming back into play when it suits Olivia best.'

Olivia's shoulders sagged. She didn't know what to do. She'd tried to reason with them. She'd tried to push back. Maybe they were right, maybe she was a dictator. Aunt Rebecca's words echoed in her head: *Stand your ground, Olivia!*

Rebecca had fought to buy back the farm. Why? Because she knew it was important. *Maybe I don't need to borrow my moves from Ivy, but from my human family instead!*

Olivia looked at the three girls, then at Camilla. Standing up for her friend had to be the right thing.

'Haven't you ever wanted to be a little different?' Olivia asked the girls, looking them up and down for any clues that maybe they weren't so uniformly pink through and through. Her gaze stopped at a piece of shiny jewellery. Hanging from Lucrezia's neck was a saxophone charm strung along a thin silver chain. 'Like perhaps wanting to play in a jazz band?'

Lucrezia's frown softened.

The hem of Melinda's skirt was uneven and Olivia realised she must have made it herself. 'Or what about making one-of-a-kind fashion statements?' Olivia suggested.

Melinda let her arms fall to her side, dropping the hard glare at the same time.

Finally, Olivia turned her attention to Veronica. She scanned every inch of her, but couldn't spot one thing that was different. Veronica was polished from her toenails to her icy blue eyeshadow.

'Oh, give it up,' said Veronica. 'You think we can't see what game you're playing?'

Lucrezia cradled the dangling saxophone charm. 'Actually, V, I think Olivia has a point.'

'You *can't* be serious. Just because you have some stupid charm and Melinda likes to make her own outfits? Please.'

Melinda's face got red, creating an unfortunate clash with her hot-pink get-up. 'Don't call her charm stupid and don't laugh at my sewing.'

Veronica tossed her arms up. 'You guys are completely missing the point! Don't you see what Olivia's trying to do?'

'No, *you're* missing the point, Veronica.' Melinda fluttered her home-made skirt. 'I'm proud to be a little different and I like this skirt!'

Olivia whispered to Camilla and Jenny, 'Let's go. They'll never notice.'

Together, Camilla, Olivia and Jenny slinked into the assembly hall, leaving the Terrible

Trio to fight it out amongst themselves.

'That was close,' said Camilla.

'No kidding.' Olivia laughed. 'I guess there are lots of different ways to stand your ground.'

'There are, but you were amazing! You deserve a medal or something!' Olivia thought Jenny might bounce right out of her boots. 'Or better yet – you should be on the diplomatic corps!' After planning this event, Olivia was pretty sure the only thing *she* wanted to be on was a beach.

Olivia noticed the music had stopped. 'Hey, who cut the sound?' she asked, worried there might be a glitch.

The DJ picked up the microphone. 'There is going to be a short break for speeches. Everyone –' he waved – 'gather round.'

Speeches? Olivia hadn't included speeches on tonight's agenda.

'Did you know about this?' she asked, turning to Jenny.

'First I've heard of it.'

Oh no! Olivia wrung her hands. Surely nobody wanted *her* to speak . . . or did they?

Olivia let out a huge sigh of relief when she saw their head of year making her way to the stage. Ms Starling wore a bright red bandana around her neck and her hair was the slightest bit disheveled, as if she'd been taking a few square-dancing spins around the dance floor herself.

Ms Starling tapped the microphone to make sure it was working. 'Firstly, I want to thank Olivia Abbott,' she began, immediately making the temperature of Olivia's face spike to a thousand degrees. 'She has done a wonderful job pulling this event together, and on such short notice, too. The whole school is united.' Ms Starling shot a significant glance at Lucrezia, Melinda and Veronica, who were busy sulking in the corner of the hall. 'And thanks to Olivia, everyone who's anyone in Franklin Grove is here.

It's truly wonderful.' Ms Starling's eyes twinkled and she clapped for Olivia.

Soon, the whole school was joining her in applause. Whoops and cheers filled the air and the next thing she knew, Olivia's feet were lifted off the floor. Her body pitched and tottered, but then she was up, balancing on top of her classmates' shoulders and parading around the room. *This is so cool!* Olivia blinked, taking a mental snapshot. Ivy stood to the side of the hall, watching her and laughing. This was the sort of moment that Olivia wanted to remember forever.

Perched up on her friends' shoulders, the assembly hall looked magical. Glitter, hay and twinkling lights all came together to create the perfect effect. As the cheering parade circled around, Olivia saw a silhouette framed in the doorway. She cocked her head. He was the only one not joining in the festivities and yet she could clearly make out the outline of a Stetson. And there something in the way he stood – it seemed so familiar.

Olivia was momentarily blinded by the flickering on of a spotlight, which settled on the mysterious figure. Her hand flew to her mouth. *It's Jackson!*

'Oh my goodness!' Olivia tapped the shoulder supporting her. 'You've got to let me down!' Olivia scrambled to the ground and sprinted over to Jackson, throwing her arms around his neck. 'You're here! You're really here!'

'Do you think I'd miss this?' Jackson murmured into her hair. From behind his back, Jackson pulled out a pink rhinestone cowboy hat and placed it on top of Olivia's head.

She felt the rim. 'Jackson, it's absolutely perfect! How did you know?'

Jackson jerked his head over to where Ivy was still looking on, smiling in Brendan's arms.

'Have I ever mentioned I love having a twin?'

Olivia asked, pushing up on her tippy-toes to plant a kiss on Jackson's cheek.

'It was tough to keep this all from you.' Jackson straightened Olivia's hat. 'I was sure my wardrobe manager was going to give it away when I was on the phone to you while she was helping me choose your perfect Stetson.'

Olivia smacked her head. 'So it really was your wardrobe manager!'

Jackson's forehead wrinkled in the cutest way Olivia had ever seen. 'Who else would it have been?'

Olivia blushed and looked away. 'Um, I don't know,' she said quickly. 'I didn't recognise the voice, that's all.'

Jackson shrugged off Olivia's comment and laced his fingers through hers. He led Olivia out to the dance floor. The singer nodded to the other band members and they switched to a slow song. Jackson curled his arms around Olivia's waist and she pressed her cheek into his sturdy chest. Now *this* was what Olivia called 'perfect'.

She recognised the recording light glowing on Charlotte's camera. She was filming the whole thing. Charlotte wiped a tear from beneath her perfectly applied mascara. Who knew – Charlotte had a sentimental streak!

'Olivia.' Jackson's breath tickled her ear. 'I can't stay long. I managed to talk my way into one night off, but tomorrow it's back to work.'

Olivia kept swaying with the melody, enjoying the smell of Jackson's cologne and the fact that there was no telephone between her voice and his. 'I understand. I can save sadness for another day. Tonight, I'm all about the happy.'

As the last slow notes of the song faded, Ivy and Brendan made their way over. Olivia hugged her sister. Without her, this surprise wouldn't have happened.

'Er . . .' Brendan looked at Jackson. 'I think

this might be a sisters-only moment. Punch?'

Olivia nodded at Jackson and the boys went off in search of Lucrezia's famous punch recipe.

The next part was harder. 'Ivy, I know.' Olivia rested her hands on Ivy's shoulders.

'Know what?'

'I know that you might not be back after the summer. Your dad – *our dad* – he sat me down earlier today, after we were done preparing for the dance, and explained everything to me.'

Ivy slumped. 'Are you mad at me?'

'How could I be?' Olivia thought her sister needed to have a little faith. 'You're about to find out if you can become the best vampire ever. I mean, how cool is that?'

'Not as cool as having you as a sister,' said Ivy, her goth-lined eyes shining.

As everyone danced around them, the twins shared another hug, this one longer and tighter than the last. Life was changing and for the first time since they had discovered each other, Ivy and Olivia were going to be apart.

Will things ever be the same?

 TWIN TALK!

In this intimate, at-home interview, VAMP magazine's Georgia Huntingdon chats to Olivia and Ivy, a very special set of twins.

Georgia Huntingdon: Thank you so much for letting me visit today! I have to ask – did you have any clue your Transylvanian grandparents were planning to come to Franklin Grove?

Olivia Abbott: We had no idea! The first we realised was when Horatio, their butler, brought us breakfast on a tray. We were both still in our pyjamas – talk about crazy!

Georgia: I must admit that I can't quite picture the Count and Countess so far from home. I hear you took them to a – *gasp!* – diner. How did they react?

Ivy Vega: Ha! Better than you'd think. The Count was totally impressed by the smoothies and I definitely saw Grandmother bobbing along to the music. Turns out they aren't so hung up on etiquette as you'd think. Horatio was the one who was freaking out! He found it impossible to stand by and not help the staff clear up.

Georgia: If I may turn serious for a moment, could I ask about your romance, Olivia? Jackson nearly didn't make the school dance you organised, did he?

Olivia: That's true, but we have to remember – he's a Hollywood actor. He was busy promoting a film and . . .

Georgia: I know all about promotional tours. They're a nightmare! But seriously, darling . . . Didn't you feel just a tiny bit neglected?

Ivy: My sister wouldn't let anyone neglect her. Despite being so busy, Jackson made it to the dance so that that he could support Olivia. Did you see that rhinestone hat he bought her? And the cowboy boots? You tell me that's not love!

Georgia: [clearing her throat] Yes, yes. I see. Moving on . . . Olivia, how did you come up with the ranch theme for the dance? It was so original!

Olivia: It's all down to our aunt – our mother's sister. We were visiting her ranch and it just . . . I don't know . . . came to me!

Georgia: [laughing] It must have been all that fresh air! Ivy, did Brendan ask you straight away to be his date to the dance?

Ivy: Not straight away. In hindsight, I can see that he was dropping hints, but . . . I don't know. I just totally wasn't expecting anything!

Georgia: I hear he bought you a unique corsage. Can you describe it for our readers?

Ivy: It was a thistle! Honestly, he knows me better than I know myself sometimes.

Georgia: A thistle! Isn't that quite dangerous to wear?

Ivy: Not if you're careful. It was the perfect present from the perfect boyfriend.

Georgia: Are wedding bells in your future together?

Ivy: Me? In a big white meringue of a dress? That's so bunny – I don't think so! Anyway, I'm far too young to be thinking about marriage.

Georgia: Ah, yes! You have other plans. I hear that you're going to be paying Transylvania another visit. How does it feel to be on the verge of becoming a student at Transylvania's most elite academy?

Ivy: Um, well . . .

Olivia: She's absolutely delighted! I know my sister will be a star student and make the best vampire ever.

Georgia: I'm sure our readers will agree with you, Olivia. But Ivy – I can't help picking up on a spot of . . . Are you unsure about going to Wallachia Academy?

Ivy: I'm just keeping an open mind at this stage. I'm confident the academy will be everything my grandparents promise me it will be . . . [Long pause]

Georgia: Okaaaaay. One last question to you both: What's all this I hear about a royal wedding?

Ivy: We have nothing to say.

Olivia: [Giggling] No comment!

Georgia: Oh, come now, girls. We're friends! You can tell me! The rumour mill is going into overdrive. Something about a certain Transylvanian prince and a . . .

Ivy: If you want the inside scoop, you'll have to ask the prince himself – if you can get near him.

Olivia: I'm sure you understand, Georgia. It wouldn't be right for us to speak on behalf of others.

Georgia: That's very gracious of you both. So, any fat, cream-coloured envelopes arriving at your houses lately?

[Silence]

Georgia: Well, that's all for today, I think. Thank you both so much for another wonderful interview. I can't wait to hear what you have to share with us next! A tale of wedding bells, perhaps . . . ?

[More silence]

Georgia: Thank you both. Bye for now!

Olivia & Ivy: Bye, Gloria!

In the next part of VAMP magazine's exclusive series of interviews with the twins, Georgia does her best to persuade the Ivy and Olivia to share Translyvania's biggest story of the year – dare we suggest, a WEDDING?!